THE NEW GIRL'S AMISH ROMANCE
AMISH FOSTER GIRLS BOOK 4

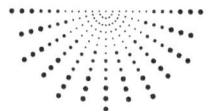

SAMANTHA PRICE

Copyright © 2017 by Samantha Price

All rights reserved.

No part of this book may be reproduced in any form or by any electronic or mechanical means, including information storage and retrieval systems, without written permission from the author, except for the use of brief quotations in a book review.

This is a work of fiction. Any names or characters, businesses or places, events or incidents, are fictitious. Any resemblance to actual persons, living or dead, or actual events is purely coincidental.

CHAPTER ONE

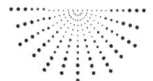

"Hello? Miss, hello?"
It took an effort for Asha to open her eyes. When she did, she saw a young man standing over her. As she blinked, he leaned closer, peering intently into her eyes. The realization hit her that she was on the ground.

"Miss, you've been in an accident, are you hurt?"

Her head was fuzzy. All she could do was stare at the man, watching his mouth open and close as though in slow motion while his words reverberated around her. She could almost see the words in the air, like butterflies swirling in a large jar. She put her hand to her throbbing head.

"Miss, are you okay?" he asked again.

"Ahh, I think I am." As Asha tried with all her

might to sit up, all went gray and everything faded into darkness.

She heard the words, "I'll call the paramedics." That jolted her back to awareness.

"No! Don't. I'm okay." With all her might, Asha opened her eyes. "Don't. I'm okay," she repeated.

"Move your toes," he ordered.

Asha moved her feet and her legs. "See? No harm done."

"I can't say the same for your car. I can call a friend to tow it to a workshop."

"Yes, please. I'm okay. I'll rest here for awhile on the ground." She closed her eyes. "Just leave me here."

"You need to be checked over. You must have a concussion, being knocked out like you were."

Asha lifted her hand and tried to grab his arm, but she had no strength. Just lifting her arm had been hard enough. "No. I can't go to the hospital."

"I can't leave you here." Asha could see him trying to decide what to do. Then he leaned over, carefully picked her up and carried her, and that was when everything faded around her once again.

When Asha opened her eyes it took awhile to remember the accident and to figure out that the young man had taken her to...wherever she was. She was in a cozy bed; the smell of freshly baked bread and freshly ground coffee met her nostrils. Wherever she was, there was a strange sense of calm.

She sat up, blinking, and figured she must be in a farmhouse. Pain gripped her and she looked down inside the white sheet wrapped around her to see a dark bruise following the line where her seatbelt had been. That seatbelt must've saved her life. Looking down at the fabric wrapped around her, she realized it was a nightgown of sorts.

Noticing a small window, she pulled her legs over the side of the bed and that's when she noticed iodine on her legs; then she saw the same on her arms. Someone had been caring for her. On wobbly legs, she managed to make it to the window and she looked out. There was nothing but fields for as far as she could see, not another house or building in sight.

She held her head and sank to the floor when she recalled speeding over the hill and swerving to avoid an Amish buggy. The next thing she remembered was her car tumbling over the side of the hill.

Thankfully, the car had come to a stop upright, she recalled, which allowed her to unbuckle her seatbelt and crawl away from the car. Then the blackness, and then that man. He must've brought her here.

Heading back to the warm bed, she was pleased that she'd gotten away from her life, away from her manager... Who was also her cheating boyfriend, Nate Berenger.

She knew she should've felt grateful to be alive, but she didn't. She didn't care. Maybe if she'd died, Nate would've been sorry for how he'd treated her, and she'd be free of pain—free from the pressure that her life had become.

Everyone on the outside looking in, thought she had the perfect life; she had platinum records and every new song became an instant hit. Her tours were always sold out, and now Nate was negotiating a movie deal where he promised she'd play opposite some big Hollywood names. No one understood the never-ending pressure that came from being on top. Sometimes she felt she was suffocating, with no relief in sight.

Closing her eyes, she remembered the scene—the last straw—that had led her to driving such a long distance that night.

Asha had walked into the busy bar, becoming annoyed that her drink wasn't waiting for her. She scanned the dimly lit nightclub for her manager and boyfriend, Nate. He was nowhere in sight. All eyes were on her from the moment she'd walked in, but that was nothing new. She was used to being the center of attention and would've been worried if she wasn't.

"Asha, can I have your autograph please?" a fan called out, waving a book and a pen.

"Not tonight, sorry. Maybe another time," Jason, Asha's bodyguard, did his best to deter the autograph hunters while bouncers moved between Asha and the anxious fans. "Sorry, Asha, we tried to make the bar for VIPs only tonight. I guess it didn't work."

"Thanks, Jason. Have you seen Nate?" Still looking into the crowd of people to see if she could spot him, Asha grew more annoyed. He'd always booked her for too many shows and didn't give a second thought to how run-down she was.

With Nate missing, Asha grew jealous. Was he with another woman? She wasn't normally a jealous person, but she knew he had a wandering eye. The fact that he was tall and handsome, with sandy blonde hair and blue eyes, and now very rich, thanks to her, didn't help matters. When the flashing lights lit up a corner of the otherwise darkened bar, she saw him...huddled next to another woman.

Anger rippled through every fiber of her being. He'd promised, sincerely she'd hoped, to be faithful and to stop flirting with other women, but that was clearly a lie. It made a fool out of her when people saw him with someone else. Everyone knew she and Nate were dating.

In a rage, she charged toward him and when she got closer, she saw that the woman he was whispering to was her best friend, Julie Rose. Both of them looked shocked and guilty when they turned to see her.

"Real best friend you are, Julie Rose! Both of you, just forget my number. And Nate, you're fired as my manager and… And everything else! I'm leaving the industry."

Nate lunged forward, sending Julie Rose flying, and grabbed Asha's arm. "Hey! Wait!"

Julie Rose stood up and laughed. "He never loved you!"

Nate was talking about contracts and how she wasn't able to fire him, but Asha wasn't listening. The two people closest to her had betrayed her. She wondered how long it had been going on between them. There was no use asking, she'd heard enough lies for one lifetime.

Asha stepped back, pulled her arm away from

Nate's grasp, and walked away. She'd call her lawyer tomorrow and get out of her contract with Nate, and find a new manager. There were two names she'd been given when she last made inquiries. Either one of them had to be better than Nate; next time she wouldn't mix business with personal relationships. She'd learned that lesson the hard way.

"Asha! Wait! Stop, I'm sorry! It won't happen again."

It was too late. Asha ran through the bar to get away and as she did, she felt all eyes on her. She ran to the elevator to get back to the safety of her room and as she waited she felt a hand slip around her waist.

"Let go of me now!" She knew it was Nate.

She screamed as he yanked her closer toward him. Without thinking, she turned toward him, balled her hands into fists and punched. Some punches connected and others flailed about in the air. Her anger was burning deep and her face burned with rage. This was not the life she'd asked for.

Then Jason, all six feet six of him, grabbed Nate. "Go, Asha," he said as the elevator doors opened.

Nate struggled, which made Jason put some kind of hold on him that sent him to the floor.

"Run, Asha, I'll be right behind you," Jason yelled.

As the doors closed, Asha heard Jason tell Nate he knew it wouldn't be long before she dumped him. At least Jason was on her side.

Once out of the elevator, she charged into her room and slumped down on the bed. As the tears rolled down her face, she was consumed with hopelessness.

She was rich and she was famous, so why was she so unhappy? From the time she'd been a young teen having singing lessons and singing into a hairbrush, she'd dreamed of this life. It wasn't supposed to be so unhappy.

All Asha could do was sob into a pillow. This wasn't the first time she had finished a show and gone to meet her boyfriend, only to find him all over someone else. Now two people had betrayed her at once. She always knew Julie Rose wanted him; seeing them kiss was no surprise, not really. They'd probably been hooking up the whole time.

They can have each other now! Asha thought.

There had to be more to life than this. The tears continued as she recalled how hard she had worked to pay for those singing lessons. Time and time again she'd heard she'd never make it. How happy she was when she finally got signed to a record label. *Easy days from here,* she'd thought. How wrong she had been.

Not content to wallow in self-pity, Asha decided to take action. She had to get away from her life and the people who surrounded her. She leaped out of bed and headed to the bathroom. Her red lipstick was smudged, and her mascara-smears gave her a panda-eyed look. She ran cold water over a washcloth and wiped off every trace of makeup. Her long blonde curls were matted and her tight white dress was now stained from tears and makeup. She pulled off the dress and threw on an old pair of jean-shorts and a t-shirt she only wore between public appearances.

Everyone always told her how beautiful she was, but what use was that? It hadn't made her happy. All the money, the makeup, the clothes, the hair, it didn't mean anything to her anymore. Neither had the thousand dollar shoes and the five star hotel rooms. Life hadn't been good before she became famous, but it was better than what she had now and there had been no pressure attached.

A change had to be made. She had to get away. Asha picked up the phone and ordered Nate's car to be brought to the front of the building. They told her it would be there in five minutes. That was just enough time for her to pack some belongings into a small bag. She'd get away by herself and Nate could explain to her fans why she quit her tour. Even though she didn't like letting her fans down, she was in survival mode. If she didn't get away, she knew she'd die. She pushed away suicidal thoughts, she wouldn't let Nate be the cause of that, but could she ever get away from the life she'd created? Everyone would know her wherever she went.

Nate burst into the bedroom and looked down at her bag.

"Where do you think you're going?"

"Away from you."

"Don't be ridiculous. I'll move into another room if that's what you want."

"I'm leaving for good. I'm getting out of the country for a while, and I'm finding peace. Now leave me alone." She'd made certain to pack her passport.

He pulled her arm. "We can work this out."

"Get away!" she hollered.

Jason walked into the room. "I'm sorry, Asha. I tried to keep him away."

"Get back, or I'll fire you," Nate said to the bodyguard.

"I work for Asha," Jason said before he dragged

THE NEW GIRL'S AMISH ROMANCE

Nate out of the room.

Asha grabbed her bag and headed to the elevator while Nate was restrained.

She jumped into the car at the front of the hotel, and sped away. Asha had no idea where she was going, hoping she'd know when she got there. When Nate finally realized she had his car, she'd be long gone. Anyway, he could go home in the tour bus, she figured.

After a couple of hours, her tears stopped flowing, slowing down to a trickle. Now she was out in the country, surrounded by trees and then fields. Time to speed up, now that she was away from the city. There'd be no police to book her for speeding in these parts. She pressed her foot to the floor.

Driving fast gave her a sense of power, of control, that she didn't have in her day-to-day life. Behind the wheel, *she* was in control and no one could tell her how to drive. When she came to a slight rise, she eased off the gas a bit. As she crested the hill, directly in front of her was a buggy with flashing lights. Asha hit the brakes and swerved to avoid it and lost control of the car. The last thing she remembered was the bite of the seatbelt as she was thrown around inside the tumbling car.

CHAPTER TWO

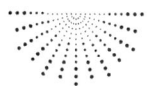

"Oh, I see you're awake! How are you feeling?"

It was an older lady in Amish clothing. She'd heard about the Amish and knew they were peace-loving and quiet people.

"Um, my chest hurts." Asha looked down at the bruise running diagonally across her chest.

"The seatbelt saved your life. You had a car accident, and my eldest son brought you back here. My name's Patsy. The doctor will be here to check on you soon."

Patsy was a small lady with a friendly face. She seemed kind. She reached over and put the back of her hand against Asha's head. *"Ach, nee.* You're quite hot. I'll fetch you a cup of hot tea and something to eat. Don't move."

"Thank you," Asha said as the old woman plumped up her pillows. "What's your son's name?"

"John Williamson. He's anxious to know that you're okay. He'll be back from milking the cows soon."

"You dressed me in this?"

The old lady chuckled. "I did. I'll wash your clothes today, but they were torn and badly soiled."

"Oh." She knew she'd had a bag in the car. "The car?"

Patsy shook her head. "John is getting a friend to help him get it towed to a workshop. John will see to it. Don't concern yourself." She turned and pointed at Asha's handbag. "There's your bag."

"Oh good. Thank you, Patsy. You're very kind." Asha put her head back on the pillow, feeling strangely peaceful.

"I'll get you that breakfast."

Patsy hurried out of the room, and Asha closed her eyes. Her thoughts stayed on the car. It wasn't her car and whatever happened to it, it'd serve Nate right. As long as they didn't trace the car back to Nate, she was perfectly safe. And with the car off the road, it would be safe if Nate had reported it as stolen.

She relaxed and listened to the strange sounds of... Of silence. She couldn't hear a thing. There had never been a more pleasing sound than none at all. Finally, she was away, "Far from the Madding Crowd," to quote the film title, away from the hustle and bustle where everything buzzed with the fast pace of life. She'd have to think of a way to prolong her stay. Patsy seemed kind; maybe she wouldn't mind if she stayed longer.

Patsy came back and placed a tray on the bed next to her. "Here you go."

There was a cup of hot tea, and toast with butter and a choice of jams.

"Thank you. This is appreciated. I'm so hungry."

"Go on, eat."

Asha smiled at Patsy who was standing there staring at her. She took a sip of tea and then spread the butter over the toast.

"Do you want me to spread it?" Patsy asked.

"That's okay."

"I didn't know how much butter you'd like. I like a lot, but many people prefer a scraping. The butter and milk are from our cows. That surprises city folk."

Asha nodded. She had just bitten into the toast and couldn't reply.

"What's your name, dear?"

Asha swallowed. It had been a long time since anyone had needed to ask her name. She was professionally known as Asha with no last name, although she was born Ashleigh Kemp. It had been Nate's idea to change her name to just 'Asha.' She tilted her head and put a puzzled look on her face. "I don't remember."

"You don't?"

"I must've bumped my head." She needed to stay somewhere where no one knew who she was. There was no way she could have a rest if anyone found out her real identity. Asha figured there was a strong chance this was her only way to escape reality. "Thank you for this." She took another bite of her toast.

"I was going to ask if you wanted to call anyone. We've got a phone in the barn, you see. Oh dear. Don't worry, the doctor will be here soon. You just finish eating, and then rest."

"You have a doctor? I didn't think Amish people used doctors or had communication with the outside world?"

"Of course we do. We're still human, we still get

sick and need medical assistance." Patsy took a little step toward her. "Do you remember the accident?"

Asha took a moment and then shook her head, wincing when that increased the headache pain.

When Patsy left the room, Asha felt bad for worrying her. She took another sip of the hot tea and tried not to worry about anything other than having a rest. After she finished all the food on the tray, she threw aside the quilt and went to look out the window again. She felt a little bit steadier now.

Looking out at the fields that stretched for miles, she saw a blue sky and a small herd of cows grazing on the grass. Asha had never seen anything more beautiful; every shade of green was featured in that field. The sky was a deep blue with not one cloud. Toward the far horizon, the sky faded to a softer, lighter blue.

Beneath her vantage point of the upstairs window, she saw a horse and buggy approach the house. It was a young man driving the buggy. Could this have been the young man, John, who'd taken care of her? She had to thank him. Her eyes were fixed on him as he jumped out of the buggy. Under his hat, she saw his hair was dark and his frame was tall and strong. This was someone she had to get to know.

She couldn't go downstairs in the sheet she was wearing. She looked around the room and saw dresses hanging on a peg. Hopefully, whoever owned the dresses wouldn't mind if she wore one of them. Quickly she slipped out of the 'sheet' and into a pale yellow dress. On the dresser, she found a brush and dragged it through her long blonde hair only to find it full of tangles. Realizing it would take some work, she sat down on the bed. Once the brush moved through her hair freely, she looked around for a mirror to see how she looked. There was none in the room. She always carried lipstick in her bag. With a clean dress, her hair brushed and a smear of lipstick, she hoped she looked presentable and ventured downstairs.

The wooden stairs creaked as she walked down them, and at the bottom, she found herself in a large, sparsely furnished living room. Hearing noises from one end of the house, she headed that way.

Suddenly the front door swung open and she jumped.

"So sorry. I didn't mean to give you a scare."

She let out a sigh, glad to see the handsome man standing in front of her. "It's okay. I wanted to thank you for bringing me here. Your mother has been so kind. You are John, aren't you?"

THE NEW GIRL'S AMISH ROMANCE

He smiled. "I am. How are you feeling?"

"Fine. Considering..."

"I'm glad to hear it. My friend towed your car and he's finding out what it takes to fix it. He can give you a quote."

"That would be good."

Asha remembered books she had read about Amish people. "I didn't think Amish drove cars. Do you?"

"My friend, Mick, is on *rumspringa*, a time of living outside the community. A rather extended *rumspringa*, it turns out. He's working as a mechanic."

Time away from Nate and the paparazzi was just what she needed. "You're very kind for helping me and bringing me here, and your mother is extremely kind also."

"It is our pleasure. It's not often that something like this happens. You are welcome to stay here as long as you need. I'm certain my mother would say the same thing."

"What are you doing out of bed?" Patsy had come from the other end of the house.

"I feel better."

"You must go back to bed until the doctor

comes." She looked at her son. "The young lady has lost her memory."

John's jaw fell open. "Really?"

Asha nodded. "I'm certain I'll be all right soon. I just need to rest."

"Back upstairs with you then. John, call the doctor and see how much longer he'll be."

"Yes, *Mamm*."

John walked out of the house and Asha stared after him.

"Upstairs," Patsy ordered.

Asha realized she had been lost in thought, and shook her head before remembering it would hurt. She wasn't used to taking orders from anyone. "Is it morning?"

"It's close to midday. Now, back upstairs with you, and lie down."

Asha smiled. "I'm going right now." Once back upstairs, Asha climbed into bed wondering whose room it was. Neither John or Patsy said anything about her wearing the dress. When she heard the door open and close downstairs, and then John's voice, she walked to the door to listen.

"They said they're too busy to come out. I'll have to take her to the doctor. Dr. Martin said to take her to the hospital, but I think she's terrified of hospitals.

I was surprised; you heard last night how scared she was of that."

"Just take her to the doctor. He should know if she's okay."

"Shall I fetch her?"

"Nee, I'll do it. You get the buggy ready."

Asha climbed back into bed and waited for Patsy to come back up the stairs.

"We have to take you to the doctor."

"That's fine. Oh, I didn't ask you. Is it okay that I wear this dress? I saw it hanging there."

"Yes. That's Becky's, my daughter. She's on *rumspringa*. Borrow anything of hers you want."

"Thank you." Asha nodded. "Yes, I've heard about that. I think I know what it is."

"John's waiting in the buggy for you."

"Okay." Asha looked around, grabbed her bag and saw her high-heeled shoes. They didn't exactly go with her outfit, but footwear hadn't crossed her mind when she'd run from Nate.

Patsy was watching Asha. "You can see if you fit into Becky's shoes. She won't mind." Patsy leaned down and handed her a pair of stockings and also retrieved a pair of lace-up black shoes.

Asha had never seen anything so ugly since she'd had to wear similar shoes for one of the schools she attended. "They look about the right size."

"Try 'em."

After Patsy placed them on the floor, Asha pushed her feet into them. "Perfect."

"Good. Then put your stockings on and you'll be ready to go."

"Thank you."

As soon as Patsy walked out of the room, Asha pulled the stockings on and then pushed her feet into the black shoes. After she'd laced them, she knew no one would know her in these clothes. Seeing a hair tie on the dresser, she grabbed it and pulled her hair back tightly away from her face. She was even more certain she was not recognizable like that.

Patsy was at the bottom of the stairs ready to escort her out to the buggy. When she climbed up next to John, she thanked Patsy again as the buggy headed away from the house.

CHAPTER THREE

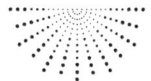

"I heard something when I was upstairs. Was I conscious last night? I don't remember anything except you after the accident. Did I say not to take me to the hospital?"

"Yes. You must've had a good bump on your head not to remember that, or who you are."

Asha sighed and leaned back in her seat. She'd never ridden in a horse-drawn buggy before and found the cool breeze on her face refreshing. It was a hot day and the scenery was so beautiful. She closed her eyes to smell the fresh air and the scent of the meadows, the trees and the wildflowers. Opening her eyes, she saw more green fields and they passed small plots of farming land.

He glanced over at her. "It's about a thirty minute ride into town. I hope you feel comfortable."

"Look. I don't think it's necessary that I see a doctor, I'm fine. Really I am."

He shook his head and looked Asha straight in the eyes. "You've no memory. I'm sure Dr. Martin is going to send you for tests."

Asha would have to delay those tests somehow. They'd want to see some form of ID and then her cover would be blown. "I suppose you're right."

As they walked through the doors of the doctor's surgery, she saw a petite young woman with strawberry blonde hair sitting behind the counter. As soon as the young woman spotted John, she jumped up to greet him.

"John! How are you? What are you doing here? Are you sick or hurt?"

Asha looked over to see John's amused face. It was clear Asha wasn't the only one who admired this handsome man.

"I'm fine, Sally. This is my friend."

John trailed off as he looked at Asha and realized he didn't know her name and, apparently, neither did she.

"Call me Jane," Asha quickly replied. John gave Asha a quick smile and turned back to Sally.

"Jane is here to see Dr. Martin."

Sally looked Asha up and down and, with a dissatisfied look and an uncertain stare, advised them to take a seat. She said the doctor would be with them shortly. Her expressions made Asha feel insecure. Did Sally know who she really was? Asha was only in her early twenties as well, and her music reached out to the young people. She tried to shake off the nerves and turned to face John.

"You don't come here much, do you?" Asha smiled at John.

"Not if I can help it."

Asha looked around the room; there were two other ladies. One old lady wore purple glasses and had pale-purple hair, and was half falling asleep, and a young-looking woman on the other side of the waiting room was reading a magazine.

They continued to wait in silence and Asha noticed Sally staring at her, and then quickly looking away so as not to make eye contact. This made Asha nervous and she was glad when the doctor opened the door and called her into his office. As Asha walked past the doctor who was holding the door open, he said hello to John.

The doctor was a small old man with gray hair, glasses and a large stomach. He had a big friendly smile that instantly made Asha feel comfortable. He advised her to step behind a curtain and change into a gown and then a nurse came into the room.

As the doctor checked her over, he asked questions about the accident. She said she didn't recall much at all. And then he mentioned that John had said she didn't remember her name.

Finding nothing physically wrong aside from bumps and bruises, the doctor advised her to get more tests done at the hospital.

"I have a fear of hospitals. Is it absolutely essential?"

"That's my advice. Of course, I can't force you to go. You can put your clothes back on and throw the gown into the hamper."

As Asha did so, she could hear him scribbling on a pad.

When she opened the curtain and sat back down, he ripped off the top sheet and handed it to her. "Take this to the hospital, if you go."

"Thank you." Asha took the piece of paper, feeling guilty for lying.

"Take a few days to rest. You've been quite

shaken up. I can see that Patsy has taken good care of your cuts and scrapes."

Asha nodded as she looked at her iodine-stained arms and legs. "Yes. She's been very kind."

"Good luck, Jane. Come back if I can help with anything more."

"Thank you, Dr. Martin." Asha walked out of the room, and John jumped to his feet. Asha paid for her visit in cash, thankful that she'd had some in the purse she came with. She also had a credit card, but if she withdrew money, someone would know where she was. There was only one thing for it, she had to make the cash last as long as possible.

"What did he say?" John asked on the way out of the building.

"He said, "Rest," and that my memory will come back in time. And if it doesn't, come back in a few weeks. If my memory hasn't returned in a few weeks, he wants me to go to the hospital and have some tests run."

John nodded. "I thought he'd have told you to go sooner."

"No. He said it's my decision, and I just need to rest."

As they made their way back to the house, Asha asked, "Was that a good friend of yours back there?"

"That's Sally. She's a friend of my sister."

"The one who's on *rumspringa?*"

"Yes. Becky. My only sister."

"She was acting so concerned, like she was your girlfriend or something." Asha giggled.

"No. There's only one woman in my life."

"Oh?"

"Sasha is her name," John replied

"That's a nice name." Asha's heart sank just a little at the thought of John having a girlfriend. Why couldn't she ever attract a nice man like John? She could tell he was good. All the men who had come her way were men like Nate. Not wanting John to notice her disappointment, she asked, "I suppose she's Amish too?"

"I guess. In a way... She is now."

Asha frowned at him and his stumbling answer to her simple question. "What do you mean?"

He smiled. "Sasha is my horse. She's beautiful, isn't she?" He nodded to the buggy horse.

"She certainly is." Asha giggled as she admired the gray horse with dapples on her rump, and her long white mane and tail. "She's such an unusual color."

"I love horses, and she's the best one I've had."

"It must to nice to be around animals all day, feeding them and looking after them."

"Do you think you've got family looking for you? Should we stop by the police station? They might have reported you missing."

"No! I'm sure that's not the case. I mean, I don't feel I'm being missed by anyone." She looked down at her finger and then held out her hand toward him. "As you can see, I'm not married. There's no ring on my finger. And I'm older than eighteen, so I'm not a child."

He nodded. "I guess you're right."

When they arrived back at the house, John took care of the horse while Asha went back inside the house. She was met at the door by Patsy.

"What did Dr. Martin say?"

"He said to rest, and if I still don't have memory in a few weeks I should go to the hospital and have some tests run."

"I'm glad you're okay. Sit down on the couch and I'll make you a hot cup of tea."

Asha sat down and wondered where she could stay. She then got up and followed Patsy into the kitchen.

"Patsy—"

Patsy swung around and hurried to pull out a chair. "Sit."

"Thank you." As she sat, she said, "I wonder if

there might be a bed and breakfast I might be able to stay at for a few days, maybe a couple of weeks?"

"You could've stayed here but with my four boys, it wouldn't be a good idea." She spun around leaving the water running into the kettle. "There's the Grabers. They had three foster children and now they only have two, so I know they've got room."

Patsy turned off the tap.

Asha didn't like the sound of that. She would've preferred somewhere she wouldn't have to interact with people. "I don't want to put anyone out."

"You wouldn't be."

After Patsy put the kettle on the stove, she sat down at the table. "I'll call them today and if they say it's okay, I'll have John take you there tomorrow." Patsy leaned forward. "Don't worry, you'll like them. Everyone likes the Grabers."

Asha smiled and nodded, figuring she might be harder to find deep within the Amish community. At a bed and breakfast, it'd be easy for Nate to find her, as she'd have to show ID and pay with a credit card.

"Thank you. I'd appreciate that."

"They've got a double wedding coming up soon. Their last two girls are marrying."

"At the same time?"

"Yes. And both are marrying lovely young men. And if I'm right, that means their house will be empty."

"As long as I'm not intruding. I don't want to bother anyone."

"Just let me speak with them after we have a cup of tea." Patsy stood up when the kettle whistled.

While Asha sat at one end of the kitchen at a long wooden table, she took a moment to have a look around the room. The floor was gray linoleum with a pattern of small tiles, the kitchen cabinets were also gray and there was one sink and one small stove. Near the stove was a wooden island counter, and against the wall there was a fridge, which she knew had to be powered by natural gas or propane.

Patsy placed tea in front of her and a plate of cookies.

"These look delicious," Asha said reaching for one.

"If the Grabers can take you, I'll make up a suitcase for you of Becky's clothing since you don't have anything of your own here. Becky won't be back for months."

"I didn't even think of that. Thank you."

"I try to be a practical person."

Asha munched into the cookie. In the past she always had to watch what she ate, but now she didn't care. The cookie was as good as it looked. "Did you make these?"

"I had a visitor yesterday who brought those ones. I make cookies about once a week. I have to fill my boys up with something. You should see how much they eat."

"I guess they need a lot when they're growing, and I suppose they work hard."

"They do." Patsy took a sip of tea.

Asha stood up suddenly. "Oh, such a pretty colorful bird was just sitting at the window."

"We get so many pretty birds here. John's got feeders by the barn."

After Patsy talked about birds, they exchanged small talk for some time. Then Asha offered to wash the dishes, but Patsy wouldn't hear of it.

"Sit and have a rest," Patsy insisted.

"I think I just need a bit of fresh air."

"There's a chair out on the porch."

"Okay." When Asha headed outside, she heard singing. She walked down the porch steps following the sound that drew her toward the barn.

Was that John singing? When she got to the barn,

she saw that it was John, cleaning out one of the buggies while he sang.

She was taken aback by the power and beauty of his voice, and closed her eyes to enjoy it more. The song continued and then stopped abruptly. Suddenly she opened her eyes to see him looking at her.

CHAPTER FOUR

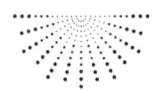

"Oh, I didn't mean to interrupt. You have a beautiful voice. What is that song? I've never heard singing like that before."

"It was one of our hymns in German."

"I would love to listen more."

He laughed. "I don't think I can sing with you looking at me. I'd like to ask you a few questions if that's okay?"

"Sure; no worries."

John walked over to the hay and pulled out a bale for Asha to sit on. After she sat down, he pulled one out for himself and sat opposite. A cat sprang onto her lap, causing Asha to yelp in fright and the cat to jump off just as fast as it had come.

"That's only Paws."

"I like cats, but I didn't see him coming. Can I pat him?"

"Sure. He's one of our barn cats. We've got three who stay in the barn and spend most of the day catching mice. If they're not doing that they're sleeping in the sun somewhere."

"He... so this one is a male?"

"Yes."

"I thought he was. He looks like a boy. Maybe it's because he's so big." Asha walked over to the cat and leaned down to pat him. He purred, curling around her legs.

"Pick him up if you want. He likes to be petted. He'll take all the attention you can give him."

Asha picked him up and sat back down with him in her lap. "He's a heavy boy."

"Yeah, he's a big cat." While the cat sat in her lap, John asked, "How are you feeling after seeing the doctor?"

"I'm feeling okay, just a little headachy and sore from the seatbelt, but I'm sure that'll go with some time and fresh air."

"Surely you have someone who will be looking for you?"

"I… I don't remember who I am."

"I know, but I think if we let the police know, then—"

"I don't remember where I came from, but I feel like I have been alone and that no one will be looking for me. Your mother says she's going to call the Grabers to see if I can stay there."

John drew his head back. "I was hoping you'd be able to stay here."

Asha remained silent. She'd prefer to stay there too. "Your mother mentioned your brothers. Will they be home soon?"

"Later. They're with my uncle today. They'll be home in time for dinner. If you do end up staying with the Grabers, would you mind if I visit you?"

"I'd like that very much. And I'll have to find out where my car is."

"I'll take you there in a few days. Where were you going in such a hurry when you nearly ran me off the road?"

"I don't remember." Asha needed to change the subject. "Is it hard to live without electricity?"

He smiled. "I've never lived *with* it, so I can't say. If you're wondering, we don't have electricity because that would be allowing the outside world into our lives. We prefer things to stay as they are.

We don't want TVs or video games because that takes away from the family."

Asha nodded. "I can see the sense in that." If Asha had a family she would've wanted to spend time with them. Jess was the only family she had ever known, and neither of them had experienced what they considered a real home. She felt a pang of anxiety, thinking that her sister had no idea where she was.

"There you are," Patsy said as she walked into the barn. "I'm going to call the Grabers."

John stood and Asha stayed seated, as the cat had gone to sleep on her. "Er, well, I'll go sit on the porch." She held onto the cat, lifting him as she stood up, and then placed him where she'd been sitting.

"Good idea," Patsy said while reaching for the phone on the wall.

Asha walked back to the porch and sat down. The sun warmed her legs as she waited to find out if the Grabers had any room for her.

When Patsy came out of the barn smiling, Asha guessed she'd heard good news.

"They said you're very welcome to stay with them. John can take you there tomorrow."

"Good. Thank you."

"Now you sit out here and rest. Close your eyes and something might come to you."

"Okay." Before too long, Asha found herself restless and made her way back to the barn, where she spent most of the day talking to John as he worked on the buggies and cleaned and oiled the leathers.

When the sun was getting low in the sky, Asha went back to the chair on the porch. She watched as a buggy came into the yard and stopped near the barn. Three young men jumped out and started walking toward the barn.

John stepped outside the house and said to her, "My brothers."

Asha felt nervous to meet these new people, until a sense of calm come over her as she reminded herself how lovely and kind John and his mother had already been to her.

"Are you sure it is no problem that I am staying here tonight? I hope I am not intruding."

"We can't leave you out on the street now, can we? It's no problem at all. I can show you around the farm tomorrow before I take you to the Grabers'."

The boys started toward the house.

"Are you ready? Here they come," John said.

The boys' pace slowed when they saw Asha.

"She won't bite," John said. "This is the lady who

was in the accident. Her name is Jane—that's what we're calling her. She lost her memory. The doctor said it should return within a few weeks."

The boys stopped a couple of yards away.

John continued, "She'll be staying with us tonight, and then she'll be staying at the Grabers'."

One young man stepped forward. "Allow me to introduce myself, Jane. My name is Scott. I'm sixteen and if I do say so myself, you're quite stunning." Scott's face beamed, causing Asha to giggle.

"Easy, Scottie," John warned.

Scott was taller and skinnier than John. He had light brown hair and green eyes, and had dirt on his face from where he must've been working in the fields.

"Pleased to meet you, Scott. I can tell you're quite the charmer."

"Quite the fool, if you ask me," one of the other brothers replied as he elbowed Scott, making the other brothers laugh. "My name is Brad, twenty one years old. Very nice to meet you, Jane. I hope you make a quick recovery."

Brad had more of a bulky build than the other boys, and his eyes were golden brown.

Asha smiled at Brad, but before she could reply, the smallest brother, with hazel eyes introduced himself. "And I am Toby, seventeen years old. I hope you find your stay here enjoyable."

"Thank you. It's nice to meet all of you. Everyone's been so kind and your mother has looked after me well."

The boys headed inside and Asha wondered where their father was. "Do you have a father, John?"

"Yes. He's inside. He came through the back door earlier. You were probably still sitting out here. He's a little shy and doesn't talk much. Some people think he's rude, but he's not. *Dat's* just quiet."

"I'll remember that. I'll see if I can help in the kitchen."

"*Mamm* might like some company. She likes to have women around now that Becky's gone."

Asha believed him. With all those boys around, Patsy probably was pleased to have a female in the house. Asha went inside with John, and while he went upstairs, she went into the kitchen. "Can I help you with anything, Patsy?"

"No. You have a rest and just keep me company. Everything's under control. Did you meet the boys when they came home?"

"Yes. They're lovely and polite. And so handsome." Asha sat down at the kitchen table.

"Well, they do have pleasant faces, and I'm happy they are polite."

Scott and Brad walked into the kitchen, and Scott said, *"Dat* will be down soon, *Mamm,* he's just freshening up before dinner."

Patsy looked over at her son pointing to dirt on his forehead. "Maybe you should have thought to do the same, Son?"

Brad laughed, leaving Scott with a dissatisfied look on his face. "You could've told me," he said to Brad, giving him a shove.

"It hid your ugly face, so I thought you wanted the dirt there."

"Brad! Enough!" Patsy said.

As Scott pushed past Brad, Brad hung his head. "Sorry, *Mamm.*" He yelled after his brother, "Sorry, Scott." There was no reply from Scott. "I was just having a bit of fun, *Mamm.*"

"You don't have fun at other people's expense. What will Jane think of us?"

Brad looked at Asha, and she didn't know what to do or say. "Maybe I should wash up before dinner, too?"

"There's a washroom through that door." Patsy pointed to a door off from the kitchen.

Jane headed to the washroom and washed her

hands, disappointed that there was no mirror to check her appearance. She washed her face and then dried her face and hands on a fluffy towel hanging on a hook.

When she went back into the kitchen, all the boys were sitting at the table and Patsy was pulling a large chicken from the oven.

CHAPTER FIVE

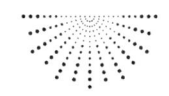

Asha went to pull out her chair, and John quickly jumped up and pulled it out for her. This set off the butterflies in her stomach again. He was so caring and so thoughtful.

"Thank you, John," Asha said with a smile.

"Ohh, 'Thank you, John.' You don't fancy John do you, Jane? I could take care of you too, you know," Scott said with desperation in his voice that once again made his brothers laugh.

"Don't mind him, Jane, he tries too hard with every girl," said Brad.

"That's why he never gets any of them," added Toby.

Asha smiled as she looked over at John; he was

trying not to laugh and Asha gathered this was so as to set a good example for his younger brothers.

"What is this fuss?" their father said as he walked into the room.

John said, *"Dat,* this is Jane."

John's father walked around and held out his hand. "Pleased to meet you, Jane. I trust you're feeling better?"

"I am; thank you," Asha said as she shook his hand.

"You can call me Joe."

"Okay, Joe."

"I trust you've been well looked after?"

Asha looked at John and was quick to assure Mr. Williamson of the hospitality she has been shown. "I am so grateful to you and your family. You have all made me feel very welcome. John has been taking care of me all day. He took me to see the doctor. I can't thank you all enough."

"Good to hear." Joe smiled and nodded at John.

The man didn't seem to be so quiet as John had said.

Patsy finished placing all the food in the center of the table. There was a lot of food. There was roast chicken, roast vegetables, fresh bread with butter and all different kinds of jam, and freshly squeezed lemonade. The aroma of the food made her tummy rumble.

John leaned over and explained, "Before we eat, we each say a silent prayer of thanks."

Asha nodded and closed her eyes along with the others. While she was there, she'd follow their customs. When she opened her eyes, she saw they all had theirs open.

"Chicken, Jane?" Patsy asked.

"Yes, please."

John placed some chicken on her plate.

"Look at you boys holding back," Patsy said with a laugh. "Normally, it's a scramble for the food."

"Don't hold back on my account," Asha said. And with that, the boys dove for the food.

"Jane, you better jump in or you'll miss out," Joe said.

"Here, I'll fill your plate," John said, taking her plate from her.

He placed it back in front of her filled with food, and then proceeded to get his own.

"This all looks so good, Patsy."

"I hope you like everything, Jane. If you don't like something, don't feel you have to eat it. There are most likely food here you haven't tried before."

"I'm sure I'll love everything." Asha had eaten

food from all over the world, and there was almost nothing she disliked.

She observed the brothers and watched as Patsy kept bringing bowls of food to replenish the table. Their accents and clothes still made her aware of how different they were, but seeing them laugh and make gentle jokes about each other made her think of her sister, Jess.

Asha felt her tummy sink when she realized that her sister would be so worried about her. Jessica and Asha were only one year apart. Jess was twenty four and had always looked out for her. They were adopted out when they were young and had no memory of their real parents. Nor did they know whatever became of them.

Their childhood was spent going from one foster-care home to another. That was why it felt so odd that Patsy had arranged for her to go to the Grabers'—another foster home. Jess and she had been lucky enough to have been kept together when they were little. As they got older, they had refused to go anywhere without the other, which made them spend most of their time in a county-run youth center.

It was having nothing to her name when she was young that had made Asha determined to achieve fame and make something of herself. She worked from age fifteen and it was then that she'd begun paying to take the vocal coaching lessons.

In the last few years, Jess had become Asha's stylist. They saw each other every day and worked well together. Jess had slightly darker hair than Asha, a light brown ashy color, and she had it cut to her shoulders with thick bangs. She never left the house without heels and always wore the tightest jeans and skimpy shirts. Not only had she made it big as Asha's personal stylist, but also with her own clothing line. They had both been determined not to let their past dictate their future.

She pushed Jess out of her mind, only because she had to. Tomorrow at the Grabers' she might be able to use their phone to call Jess and tell her she was okay.

Soon her life would go back to the way it had been, so she pretended that this was her family. This was her life, and John was her husband.

The conversation flowed over dinner, mainly with the boys making jokes. They made Asha giggle and she got to know their personalities more. She started to adore Scott as if he were her own little brother, and Todd as well. She always wondered what having a brother would feel like.

"Tomorrow, before I take you to the Grabers', I can show you around the farm. I hurt my leg in the accident, so I will be off work for a few days." John advised Asha.

"I'm sorry! I didn't know about your leg."

"It's nothing. I'm just taking the opportunity to rest," John said with a smile.

"Meaning he's faking it," Scott called out and the other brothers agreed.

Asha smiled. "I would like to learn more about your culture and lifestyle."

This made Joe sit up straighter in his chair. "You'd like to know more?"

Asha nodded.

"I'm so glad to hear it," he said with a warm smile softening his weathered face.

"Yes, and one day you might come back from the Grabers' to visit me and I'll show you how to make jam. Unless you already know?" asked Patsy.

"I would love to learn how to make jam. I've never done anything like that."

Patsy's face beamed with delight. "Good. I'll have John fetch you one day and bring you back here."

Dinner was delicious. She could tell it was all homemade. Even the butter tasted delicious. So flavorsome. The chicken was moist and the bread was soft. Asha felt her heart opening the more she spoke with the family. She enjoyed how they were relaxed and didn't appear to be worried or concerned over anything.

After dinner, Asha collected the plates to help Patsy with the dishes.

"Oh no you don't; you need to rest some more. Up to bed and we'll see you in the morning."

"Thank you, Patsy. This was a wonderful meal."

Asha looked to John who was wiping his face and hands. "Thank you, John. I have enjoyed meeting you and cannot thank you enough for your help."

John gave Asha a warm smile. After saying goodnight to the family, she was half way up the stairs when she heard a voice yell out.

"Sleep well, Jane!"

That made Asha giggle. "Good night, Scott," she said as she heard the boys cackling.

"Oooh, someone's in love," one of the brothers teased Scott.

As she lay in bed, her mind raced once again and her heart rate escalated.

The anger started inside her as she thought of Julie Rose and Nate. Feelings swirled in her head about how badly Nate had treated her. She pushed him out of her mind and replaced him with images of kind and gentle John. He was tall and friendly and so nice to look at.

And then she did her best to put all the worries out of her head before she slipped between the sheets. Even though it was still early, she welcomed the chance for sleep. It wasn't long after she pulled the quilts up around her shoulders that she fell into a deep sleep.

CHAPTER SIX

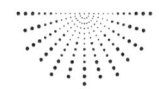

When she woke the next morning it was peaceful, with only the sound of birds singing. She dressed and went downstairs, hoping she could make herself useful before she went to the Grabers'. When she walked into the kitchen, she saw it was just Patsy there.

"Good morning, Patsy. Where is everyone?"

Patsy swung around from the stove. "Good morning. They have all left long ago except for John. He's in the barn or doing something with his horse."

"I was hoping to get up early enough to help you with the breakfast."

Patsy chuckled. "You would've had to get up a lot earlier to do that. Can I make you some pancakes?"

"Oh, yes please."

"Take a seat."

Asha pulled out a chair and sat down at the table. "Have you always lived here? I mean have you always been Amish?"

"Yes, both Joe and I were born into the faith."

Patsy poured the pancake batter into the hot frying pan and Asha took delight in listening to it sizzle.

"Coffee?"

"I'd love a cup. Just black with no sugar."

Patsy made a funny face. "How can you have it black and with no sugar?"

"Well, that answer came out automatically. I think that's how I normally drink it."

"At least you can remember some things. Have you had any other flashes of memory?"

She shook her head. "No."

"Perhaps God wants you to stay in the community for awhile," Patsy said with laughter in her voice.

"Perhaps that's true. I'm looking forward to meeting the Grabers."

"You'll like them, as I told you yesterday." Patsy placed a mug of coffee in front of her. "The beans are freshly ground."

"I can smell it. It's very strong."

"If it's too strong, I'll put a little hot water in it. Or you should try a little milk."

Asha sipped the coffee. "It's perfect. Just right."

"Good." Patsy turned her attention back to the pancakes and flipped three pancakes over.

John walked into the kitchen and sat down. "Good morning, Jane."

"Good morning."

"Good idea. I need some coffee too." He sprang to his feet and poured himself a cup.

When he sat back down, Asha asked, "Are you still going to have time to show me over the farm?"

"We'll have plenty of time. Do you want to go to the Grabers' with me, *Mamm,* when I'm taking Jane?"

As Patsy slid the pancakes onto a plate, she said, *"Jah,* I'd like to visit them."

"Good. Shall we leave at eleven?"

"Okay." Mrs. Graber put a plate of pancakes in front of Asha.

"Thank you." There was already maple syrup and butter in front of her.

"Would you like cream or jam or anything else with the pancakes?" John asked.

"No, thank you. I just like butter on my pancakes, nothing else, and this butter is so nice."

"It's from our cows," John said.

"I know. Your mother was telling me that yesterday."

After breakfast, John walked over part of the farm with Asha.

"How big is it?" she asked.

"It's nearly eighty acres."

Asha giggled. "I've really got no idea how big that is. Is that big, or average?"

"It's fairly average around these parts. Most of us in the community try to grow our own food, as much as we can anyway, and we also trade with each other."

"That sounds like a good idea."

"And what's left over generally ends up at the markets."

John showed her their five cows, the chickens, the goats and the few sheep.

"How many horses do you have?"

"We have four buggy horses. One's getting old so we don't use him much anymore; he's pretty much just put out to pasture. That's him over there."

Asha looked to where he was pointing. "The black one?"

"That's him. Do you want to go over and say hello?"

Asha shook her head. "No. I'm a little scared of horses. They're so big."

"He's as quiet as any horse can be, so he's a good horse to help you get over your fears."

"I think my fear is there for a reason — to keep me alive."

"Trust me. You can stroke his nose; it's very soft."

"Okay, but if he charges at me, I'm pushing you in front of me so he'll get you first."

"That sounds fair."

They set off into the pasture, and the black horse stopped eating grass and watched them approach.

"What's his name?"

"Blackie."

Asha shook her head. "That's original."

John laughed. "My father let me name him. I was only five at the time. What else would a five-year-old name a black horse? Now I can think of some better names, like Shadow or Midnight, but he'll always be Blackie."

As they walked closer, Asha walked slower and John turned around and looked at her, following a few paces behind.

"Don't tense. He'll sense it and think there's

danger around, or you're going to hurt him. Just relax."

Asha nodded and did what he suggested and when she drew level with John, they continued walking toward the horse.

The horse took a step to them.

"He's interested, curious enough to come and say hello."

John put his hand out for the horse to sniff.

"Now you do the same," he instructed.

She put her hand out and the horse sniffed her too, placing his nose on her palm. "You're right, his nose is so soft."

"Now do you feel brave enough to touch his nose like this?" John lightly stroked Blackie's nose.

"He likes it."

"Go on. Try it."

Asha did what John said.

"Aren't you glad you did this?"

"I am."

"Well, that might be enough for one day. If we don't leave at precisely eleven *Mamm* will get really upset. She is a stickler for being on time."

As they walked back to the house, Asha said, "Thank you for showing me the farm. It must be lovely here with the animals, and so relaxing. I've got an idea that my life before the crash was anything but relaxing."

"I hope your memory starts coming back soon."

Asha nodded. "Me too. I'm sure it will."

When the house came into view, they saw Patsy waiting in the chair on the porch. She had a black cape around her shoulders and a black over bonnet on her head.

John said, in a low voice, "What did I tell you? I pulled the time of eleven out of my head and the Grabers aren't even expecting us at any particular time, but because I said eleven it must be eleven."

Asha giggled.

When they got closer, Patsy stood up. "Jane, I've packed you a bag."

Remembering Patsy had said she would pack her bag of her daughter's things, Asha said, "Thank you very much, that is very kind of you. I'll bring them back when I'm ready to leave."

"No hurry."

"Are we late, *Mamm?*"

"It is five minutes to go before eleven o'clock and you haven't even hitched the buggy yet."

"I'm doing that right now."

While John headed to the barn, Patsy said, "You can wait next to me on the porch here, Jane."

CHAPTER SEVEN

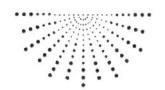

On the way to Gretchen and William Graber's home, Patsy told her as much as she could about the family.

"For the past few years, Gretchen and William have had three girls living with them. Let me see now. There was Elizabeth, and Tara, and Megan. I would guess they were all with the Grabers for five or six years. Wouldn't you say so, John?"

John shrugged. "I thought it was more like ten or something."

"Anyway, now Elizabeth is married to Joseph and Tara married Caleb not so long ago."

"Didn't you say there was a double wedding coming up?" Asha asked.

"I did, yes. The double wedding is Megan's and

Stephanie's. Megan is marrying a man called Brandon. He used to be an *Englisher,* but he's taken the instructions and now he's living with an Amish family until they marry."

"How lovely. He converted for her?"

"That's right," Patsy said.

"And who are Megan and Brandon getting married with?"

"Gretchen's niece, Stephanie. Now she was a little bit of a handful, in and out of trouble. Her father sent her to live with Gretchen, his sister. While Stephanie was there she was reacquainted with Jared who she met while she was staying with Gretchen years ago. And now Stephanie and Jared are getting married. The two girls became quite close and Stephanie decided to continue living with Gretchen and William. Stephanie's family had left the Amish years ago, but now she's back with us."

"And when is the wedding?"

"The wedding is not this coming Thursday but the Thursday after that," John said.

"It's very kind of them to let me stay there."

"You'll fit in nicely with the girls. You're around about the same age. Do you remember how old you are?"

Asha shook her head at the woman who was turning around from her front seat to look at her.

Patsy turned back around. "I'm sure your memory will come back to you soon."

"And if it doesn't, I'll take you to the hospital for those tests, Jane."

"Thank you, John."

"And I'll come back and visit you soon."

"I'd like that."

When they stopped outside the Grabers' house, Asha was surprised how small it looked compared to the Amish farmhouses that they had passed. Patsy took her by the arm and led her inside to meet everyone.

A woman appeared at the door. Asha saw right away that Gretchen Graber had a lovely kind face and immediately made her feel at ease. This wasn't like the foster homes she and her sister had been in and out of. She was certain these people would be different.

"Welcome, Jane."

"Thank you so much for having me. I hope I'm not putting you out with the two weddings coming up."

"We've always got room for one more. You can

call me Gretchen or Aunt Gretchen as the other girls call me."

"Okay." Asha glanced around at John who was doing something with his horse.

"It's just me at home. I sent the girls shopping. When they're at home, Megan is out somewhere in the fields. She has beehives that keep her busy, and Stephanie's off somewhere doing something." Gretchen gave a little laugh. "I fixed us up some tea."

Asha and Patsy followed Gretchen into the living room where there was a small table covered with cakes and cookies, and a teapot with several cups around it.

John stuck his head through the door. "Hi, Gretchen. Is Jared around?"

"No, he's off with William. You'll have to join us ladies for tea and cake." He stepped through the door rubbing his hands together. "I won't say no to that."

After everyone was seated with a cup of tea, Gretchen said, "Jane, Patsy tells me that you had a dreadful accident and you've lost your memory."

"That's right. I don't remember who I am or where I come from. The doctor said my memory should return soon, and if it doesn't I have to go to the hospital. I think I just need some peace and quiet and then everything will come back."

"Yes, I hope so."

"I nearly collided with John's buggy," Asha added.

"You wouldn't remember, but you clipped the back of it."

Asha gasped. "I'm sorry. I didn't know."

"I saw you coming when I heard the car in the still night, and I thought you were going to run into me so I leaped out of the buggy."

Patsy said, "John! You shouldn't have done that. You could've been badly hurt! She could have run over you."

"God was watching over me."

"I'm sorry about that—your leg and your buggy. Let me know how much it costs to fix."

"Don't worry about that. It was just some scratches and I can fix it. Anyway, you've got your car to worry about."

"It sounds like God was watching over the both of you," Patsy said.

Asha nodded.

"Do you have any belongings, Jane?" Gretchen asked.

"I packed her a bag of Becky's clothing."

John said, "I left that in the buggy. I'll get it before we leave."

"Help yourself to the cake and cookies, don't be shy, Jane."

"They do look delicious." Asha leaned forward and took a chocolate chip cookie, took a bite and then balanced the rest of the cookie on the saucer that held the teacup.

After they drank their tea, it was time for Patsy and John to leave. Asha was nervous to see them go.

John hurried and brought the small suitcase, putting it next to them on the porch. "I'll see you soon, Jane, and hopefully I'll have news about your car."

"That will be good. Thanks, John."

As the buggy drew away from the house, she stood alongside of Gretchen watching them.

Asha hated talking about money; Nate had always done the negotiations on her behalf, but she knew she had to raise the issue. "Gretchen, I just want to let you know that I don't expect to stay here for free. As soon as I know who I am I will have access to my bank account, no doubt, and then I can pay you for staying here."

"No need to worry about that. Whenever you're ready you can contribute for the food, but only if you want to." The woman smiled kindly at her.

Asha made a mental note to pay the woman

handsomely when she got back to reality.

"Is there anything I can do to help with the wedding or anything?"

"Not right now, but there will be in the coming days. It's always good to have an extra pair of hands about the place. You could help me now by clearing the dishes if you feel up to it."

Together they carried the dishes to the sink. Gretchen placed the uneaten food away while Asha did the washing up.

"You've been a foster parent for a while?" Asha asked.

"For quite some years. William and I could never have children of our own and we knew that was because God had a plan. There are so many children out there who need love and attention. If we'd had our own, then those who came to us might have gone where they were neglected or uncared for. God has had His hand on every child who came to us."

"And the last two girls you have here are getting married? And then you and William will be on your own?"

"Megan was a foster child of ours, but Stephanie is my niece."

"Oh, that's right. I remember Patsy telling me that on the way here."

Asha could see how genuine Gretchen was about looking after foster children and she wasn't doing it for the money the government gave her to do so, as she suspected with some of the foster parents she'd been placed with. Most of her experiences had been bad.

"And I suppose you don't remember how old you are?"

"No, I don't."

Gretchen studied her face. "It's hard to say. You've got beautiful skin, and you're a very pretty girl. I would say you're in your early twenties somewhere."

"Possibly," Asha said. "So your niece was an *Englischer?*"

"That's right."

Asha was now worried that Stephanie, Gretchen's niece, might recognize her.

"Her father is my brother and he left us many years ago. He turned to me when he couldn't control Stephanie. She's lively, but Jared has calmed her. They're truly good together and well suited."

When they heard a buggy, Gretchen rushed to the window and looked out. "Here the girls are now. Stephanie and Megan. Come out and I'll introduce you to them."

CHAPTER EIGHT

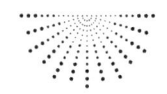

Asha knew full well that this could all be over soon if one of the girls recognized her, but would anyone know her in these clothes and without makeup? She followed the small Amish woman out to the porch.

"Where are they?" Asha asked.

"They're in the barn now. They won't be long."

Asha couldn't see them, but now she could hear them talking and giggling. She hoped she would get along with them. Several minutes later, two girls wearing Amish clothing walked toward the house.

"Girls, this is Jane. The girl I told you about who'll be staying with us for a while. Jane, this is Stephanie and this is Megan."

The girls said hello to one another.

Stephanie stepped forward. "You look a lot like Asha. Except her face is slightly different."

"Who's Asha?" Megan asked.

"Don't worry about it," Stephanie said shaking her head.

Phew, that was a close call! "I hear you're both getting married soon, and at the same time?" The girls looked as though they were still teenagers.

Stephanie said, "I'm marrying Jared, and Megan is marrying Brandon."

Megan nodded. It was clear she was the quieter of the two.

"Where are my groceries?" Gretchen asked.

The two girls looked at each other and then burst out laughing.

Stephanie said, "We left them in the buggy."

"Well, go and get them."

"Do you need help?" Asha asked, trying to make friends with them.

"Yeah, okay. We've got quite a few bags," Stephanie said.

Asha walked with the girls around the corner of the barn. It opened up to a large area where two buggies were kept.

"Is that too heavy?" Stephanie asked after she handed Asha two bags.

"No, I can carry more."

Stephanie gave Megan some bags and then Asha another one. Then with their hands full, the three girls walked to the house.

"How long are you staying with us, Jane?" Megan asked.

"Maybe a couple of weeks. I'm trying to get my memory back."

"You don't remember anything?" Stephanie asked.

"No, I don't. I remember a little before the accident and that's it. The doctor said I should get the memory back over a short time."

"You don't remember your family or anything?" Megan asked.

"Nothing." Asha thought it might be a good idea to block out the past. What if she had really lost her memory and didn't know who she was, and she wasn't Asha, the famous singer. If she had really lost her memory, she could have a chance to start her life over again. Who would she become? One thing she knew for certain was that she didn't want to be famous.

The girls made their way into the kitchen and placed the bags on the wooden table.

"Stephanie, you can help me in here and Megan,

you can take Jane to the spare room and help her settle in."

"*Jah, Mamm,*" Megan said, while Stephanie didn't look too happy to be the only one helping in the kitchen.

As Megan was walking down the hallway carrying the small bag, Asha said to her, "You called Gretchen, '*Mamm?*'"

"Yes, that's how we Amish say Mom."

"You feel that close to her that you call her that when she's your foster mother?"

"Yes, I've called them *Mamm* and *Dat* for a long time. I've never known any mother or father. They're the only ones I'll ever have and they're the closest people to me. I went from foster home to foster home before I came here." She nodded to a room, then walked toward it and pushed the door open. "This is your room."

Megan's story was similar to her own. "What was it like in the foster homes?"

Megan placed the bag down and sat on the bed and Asha sat next to her.

"No one wanted me. I can't even count how many foster homes I was in. And then for a long time I just remained unclaimed, uncared for in the orphanage. No one wanted to adopt me because I was sick all the time when I was young. And I don't know why that was. I must have had something that I grew out of."

"Unless you were allergic to something."

"If I was allergic to something, I've never found out what it was."

Asha said, "It was a good thing you came here to live with Gretchen, then."

"God had his hand on me."

"Were you Amish before you came here?"

"No, none of us were. Stephanie is Gretchen's niece and her father is Tom. He was raised Amish and then he left the community so Stephanie was raised an *Englischer* for most of her life."

"That's interesting," Asha said even though she'd heard that three times now.

"I can't even ask you any questions because you can't remember anything."

"That's right. It's quite a strange feeling not to have any past. So I don't know who I am." She was lying about not remembering, but she wasn't lying about not knowing who she was.

"I used to think that if my mother ever came to find me that I would know who I was, but then I realized that you are who you are and it's got nothing to do with your parents. We are all individuals. Brandon was looking into finding my mother for me for a while, because I thought I wanted to know, and then I had to tell him to stop."

"Why?" Asha asked.

"If I found out she was dead, I thought it would be too much pain to deal with, and if she is alive, why hasn't she ever come to find me?"

"So you feel more comfortable not knowing?"

"I guess so." Megan nodded. "Now you know all about me."

Asha wished she could share her story, too. As Megan said, it shouldn't matter who your parents were or where you came from. Asha too had decided not to find out more about her parents. Maybe one day she'd want to know, but for the past few years she'd been too busy pushing herself to get to the top of the music industry to worry about her parents and why they'd given her and her sister away.

After having a nice talk with Megan as they unpacked her bag, Megan went to help with the meal while Asha stayed in the bedroom.

Asha sat on the bed looking around the bare room. On the walls there was nothing but a small sampler with cross-stitching that read, "God is Love." The bed seemed comfortable enough and there were two pillows on it, which made her happy.

Her thoughts soon turned to Jess. The Grabers surely had a phone in their barn, the same as at Joe and Patsy's house, but how was she going to get to it? She knew she was going to have to wait until tomorrow. She couldn't risk sneaking out at night in case someone saw her. In the day, it would be much easier to say she was going for a walk and then she could slip into the barn and make that telephone call.

Hearing the lively chatter from the kitchen, she headed back to join them. Soon she was sitting down with the girls as they peeled vegetables for the dinner. The conversation was fun and lively and these girls didn't have a care in the world. Asha knew she had to make her life like theirs. She'd gone against the odds to become a famous singer; she could do it again and have a different life.

Soon William Graber and Jared arrived home for dinner. Jared was clearly taken with Stephanie and could hardly keep his eyes from her. It was sweet to see young people in love, Asha thought.

After dinner the girls pulled their wedding dresses out to show Asha. They had matching blue dresses that ended below the knee, white organza capes, prayer caps and aprons. The clothes they were wearing to their wedding were pretty much the same as they wore every day, just a little bit fancier and brand new.

That evening they hand sewed the dresses of their attendants, who were also wearing matching blue dresses but in a lighter shade.

The girls explained to Asha that they had sewn most of the dresses on a friend's gas-powered sewing machine, and they were only sewing the hems by hand.

When William and Gretchen went to bed, Asha stayed up with Stephanie and Megan.

"Do either of you work?" Asha asked.

"I work part-time at a coffee shop, and Megan sells her honey and works for someone at the farmers markets."

"Oh yes, I've heard about your bees, Megan."

"Really?"

"Yes. I think Patsy told me that you keep bees."

"I can show them to you tomorrow."

"There's not much to see. They are just boxes with bees buzzing around," Stephanie said.

"I'd love to have a look at them," Asha said.

"I have to leave for work really early in the morning but I can show you when I get home."

"Good. I'm not going anywhere as far as I know." Asha had already told them over dinner about the accident and her car rolling down the hill after clipping the back of John's buggy. "John said he would come and get me and then we'll both go and see about my car."

"That's one thing I miss — cars," Stephanie said. "Buggies are so slow."

Megan said, "Now that you're in the community, Stephanie, you don't have to hurry anymore."

"Everything's a lot slower," Stephanie said.

"What else do you miss?" Asha asked Stephanie.

"Nothing else. I would miss Jared if he wasn't here, but now since he's in the community and I'm in the community, I have everything I want."

"That must be a very nice feeling," Asha said.

CHAPTER NINE

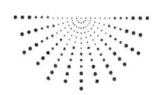

The next day, after an early breakfast, everyone except Gretchen left for work and Asha excused herself after helping clean the kitchen, saying that she needed to get some fresh air and would go for a short walk.

As soon as she slipped through the door of the barn, she spotted the phone. Taking a deep breath, she picked up the receiver. She wasn't exactly sure what she was going to tell her sister. She knew Jess would be an absolute mess and looking for her everywhere. It only took a few rings before she answered.

"Hello?" a nervous voice answered the phone

"Jess, it's me."

"Where are you?" Jess replied in a panicked voice.

"I've had to get away for a while."

"Are you okay?"

"Yes."

"Why are you whispering? Whose number is this?"

Oh no! She hadn't blocked the caller ID. "Jess, you must not call back on this phone. I'm staying with some people and they've got no idea who I am. Promise me?"

"Okay. Just tell me where you are."

"I can't. I'm okay. Don't tell anyone I called you."

"Nate's been frantically worried. He's about to put out a press release."

Asha sighed. "Okay. Tell him I called you and I'm okay. I'm taking a vacation."

"Just tell me where you are."

"I can't. You've got to trust me. I'll call you back in a day or two. Just don't tell Nate where I am."

"You haven't even told me."

"I wrecked Nate's car and—"

Jess gasped.

"I was just banged up, nothing broken or anything. A nice man found me, an Amish man. I'm staying with his family. They are lovely and they're letting me stay here until I feel better."

"What? Have you gone mad? Do you know how

sick and worried I've been, thinking my little sister has been abducted, if not killed, and this whole time you've been more than okay?"

Asha understood Jess's point, but for the first time ever, she didn't let the guilt overtake her. For once she was putting herself first. For once, she was doing what she wanted to do and not living her life to please others while sabotaging herself.

"I understand and I am sorry, Jess. I'm not exactly 'more than okay,' though. I'm still recovering from the car wreck, and what came before it. Just tell Nate I'm taking time off. I saw Nate making out with Julie Rose, and that was the last straw. I had to run. I can't go back to him, or to that lifestyle. I need time to sort myself out."

"Asha, you've got commitments. You've always known what Nate was like. And I told you not to trust Julie Rose."

"I love you. I'll call again soon. Remember what I said, just give me some time."

"No, Asha, you don't understand. Nate has gone mad; he's gone crazy. He's drugged himself and been in the hospital because he was so stressed and worried about you. He only woke up yesterday and he has to be heavily medicated because when he remembers, he goes crazy again. It's weird, it's like you were a drug to him. He needs you."

"Not badly enough to be faithful to me. And I don't need him. This time I need to look after myself." Asha couldn't believe what she was hearing. Sure, it would've been stressful for him to cancel the tour and she guessed he would've had to make an announcement that she was ill. That would've created stress for him.

"Ash, you there?"

"If he cared about me, he wouldn't treat me like that. I've got to go, Jess, love you." Asha replaced the receiver. She could've done without knowing anything about Nate, and it most likely wasn't true anyway. Nate would've made her sister say all that just to worry her.

Asha walked out of the barn and headed toward the fields. Maybe a walk in the fresh clean air would help to clear her head and her emotions. When she heard a buggy she stopped still, and then turned around to see John's buggy heading toward the house. She walked over to meet him.

"Hello," she said, trying to hide her smile. She was pleased to see him.

He stopped the buggy. "Hello, Jane. How are you

on this fine morning?" A smile twitched at the corners of his lips.

"I'm doing well. I was just about to take a walk in the fields."

"My mother sent me over here to see you."

Asha had hoped that John was there because he wanted to see her.

"She's got it into her head that you're going to help her make jam."

Asha giggled. "She did mention something about that."

"Well, what do you think? Do you think Gretchen will mind if you spend the day at my house? I think my mother misses my sister. She said it was nice to have some female company around."

"I'll see. I'll just ask Gretchen if she'll mind. I'm sure she won't."

Asha hurried into the house and once she talked to Gretchen, she grabbed her bag and shawl and headed out to John's waiting buggy.

"She doesn't mind at all."

"Well, let's go," he said, letting his smile light up his face.

Asha climbed up next to him. "Gretchen dropped a hint about bringing some jam back to her."

John chuckled. "I'm sure that can be arranged." He turned the horse around and started back down the driveway. "So, what do you think of the Grabers?"

"The girls are really nice. And so are Gretchen and William, of course. I've gotten to spend some time with Stephanie and Megan." Asha wondered why John hadn't gotten together with either one of those girls. Perhaps she might find out one day soon. She didn't know him well enough to ask him.

"Before I came here, I stopped by to talk to my friend—the mechanic. He has to order some parts for your car and then the car will need the dents pounded out before they touch up the paint. That can all be done at the same place he works."

"That sounds expensive."

"He'll do a quote."

"That's fine."

"It's Saturday today so he's not working, but did you want to stop there and talk to him about your car or anything one day early next week?" He glanced over at her.

"That would be good, if you don't mind."

"I'd be happy to take you there."

"Good."

"So, how are you feeling?"

Asha rubbed her shoulder. "The bruise from the

seatbelt is going down a bit and my scrapes are healing well, but I haven't remembered anything yet and there's still a bit of headache."

"My brothers are all home today."

"That's right, it's Saturday."

"They work most Saturdays, but they're not working today because we're preparing the house for our meeting there tomorrow."

"At your house?"

"Yes. We have our meetings every second Sunday, and we take it in turns to host them at our houses."

"I see. And tomorrow is your turn."

"That's right."

When they got back to the Williamsons' house, Asha felt more comfortable being there, almost as though it was home. He stopped the buggy behind the barn.

"You go on ahead. I'll unhitch the buggy."

"Okay." Asha walked toward the house, and then stopped to pat the large cat she'd met. "Paws," she remembered "Ah yes, that's your name, isn't it?"

He purred loudly in response.

When she walked further, she spotted John's brothers carrying wooden chairs and tables from a big wagon into one of the barns closest to the house.

CHAPTER TEN

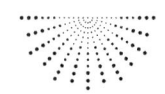

Asha wandered over to John's brothers to watch what they were doing. Scott spotted her as she approached, and a large smile creased his face.

"Jane! My dearest Jane. How are you this fine morning?"

Scott made Asha laugh at his eagerness to please. "Hi Scott. I'm fine, thank you. How are you?"

"Fine."

"What are you guys moving all this furniture for?"

"The meeting is here tomorrow."

"And you have it in the barn?"

"Yes. The house can't hold that many people."

Asha peered through the large barn doors to see

what must've been over fifty long benches. To the other side were chairs and tables. "How many people will be coming?"

"About one hundred and fifty to two hundred."

"Wow! Keep working. I'm off to help your mother make jam."

"She's excited about you helping her with the jam," Scott told her.

Asha headed to the house. As she walked through the doors, the scent of freshly baked cake wafted to her. It was her favorite smell and, she thought, just how a home should smell. "Hello," she called out.

"I'm in the kitchen, Jane."

Patsy was mixing something on the counter and turned around to face Asha.

"Hi Jane, and good morning. I'm making food for tomorrow before we start on the jam. Would you like to help mix some more cake batter?"

"I'd love to help." Asha walked over to the table. "And good morning to you, too."

"Thank you. I've already finished two. We have four more to make, including the one I'm mixing, and then we'll go on to the main meal," Patsy replied as she put the cake recipe in front of Asha. "Everything you'll need is here." She pointed to a counter covered in eggs, flour, sugar and milk. "If you could finish these, that would be a big help for me."

"Sure. Patsy, Scott told me there are over one hundred and fifty people coming tomorrow. So every time you hold church at your house, you cook for one hundred and fifty people? Alone?"

Asha saw Patsy give a small smile as she looked in her direction. "Becky always helped me before, and I'm thankful you're here today. Everyone in the community helps. Most people bring food to contribute to the meal after. But the family holding the meeting will provide most of the food. It's a blessing to have it at our house."

Patsy's dedication to her family and the Amish community was something that inspired Asha and made her start dreaming of her own family that she could care for in the same loving way. While she was here, she would learn all she could from them.

"I am looking forward to church tomorrow. I guess the Grabers would be going?"

"Yes, of course."

"Good." Asha read the cake recipe.

"I am so pleased to hear you want to come, Jane. You seem to be settling in very well."

"Patsy, I feel that I really don't want to leave here.

I fear that the life I was living before was horrible. I'm not so sure I want my memory to return."

Before the accident, she was not living like a good person, especially compared to them. She drank every night, and spent all her money as fast as she made it. She didn't care about life, she was looking for an escape in any way that she could find it, and this led her to bad lifestyle habits. A tear fell down her face and Patsy noticed, dropping everything in her hands. She walked over to Asha, wrapping her in her arms.

"Oh, dear, it's okay. The Lord teaches us not to live in fear. I'm certain everything is going to work out okay for you, my dear Jane."

Asha felt so comfortable in Patsy's arms.

"Do you want us to pray together now?" Patsy asked as she stepped back.

Asha sniffed and nodded. "I'd like that."

Patsy closed her eyes. "Thank you for bringing sweet Jane into our lives. We come before you today to pray for strength. Strength and hope for Jane and her life. We pray that she finds all that she is looking for, we pray for her health and ask you to bless our lives and restore Jane's health. Thank you, Heavenly Father, Amen."

Asha fought back more tears. She was so moved,

so touched. No one had ever prayed for her. She had goosebumps all over her body.

When Asha opened her eyes, she said, "I will pray for a family like yours one day. You are all so kind, so loving and warm. I want a house like this, I want children like yours and I want a beautiful man in my life, like your husband."

Patsy smiled at Asha. "Then say a prayer to God and He will give you what you ask for. All you have to do is believe."

There was a loud bang at the door and Patsy and Asha looked over to see that John had just closed the door with his foot.

"I'm sorry, was I interrupting something?" John asked. As he looked into Asha's face, it was clear she had been crying. "Jane, are you okay? Did you remember something?" John dropped the bag he was carrying and quickly walked toward Asha.

"I'm alright, John. No need to worry." Seeing John care so much about her made her feel happy inside.

Patsy said, "It would've been nice if you could've stayed here, Jane, but you can visit whenever you'd like. You'll be here tomorrow, too, and I have something for you."

"For me?" Asha asked.

"Jah, for you." She walked out of the room and came back holding a black book.

"A Bible?" Asha asked.

"It is." She handed it to Asha.

"Thank you. No one has ever given me anything like this."

"I thought you might like it."

John said, "Do you have a Bible, Jane?"

"No, I don't think I ever had one, but I do now," Asha said, staring at it in wonderment. What if the key to having a good life was somewhere in that book? If it was, she was determined to find it.

"You can leave it on the shelf there so it won't get jam or cake mix all over it."

"Yes, okay." Asha walked over and placed the Bible on the shelf Patsy had pointed to.

Patsy stared at John, who was still looking at Asha. "Do you plan on helping us in the kitchen today, John?"

John whipped his head around to face his mother. "I'll get out of your way."

Asha and John exchanged smiles before he left. She knew John liked her and she was pleased about it. He was a genuine man and would never treat her like Nate had. If she married a man like John, her life would be complete. In the short time she'd been with the Amish, she had come to know their world was real. Not fake, like her world that was built on falsity and vanity. No one in that world took time to care for anyone—everyone was out for themselves.

After half a day in the warm kitchen getting to know Patsy better over cooking and jam making, John drove her back to the Grabers.'

As the buggy clip-clopped down the winding narrow roads, she looked down at the Bible in her hands. "It was so nice of your mother to give me this. I shall read it tonight."

"What, the whole thing?" He laughed.

"Well, not all of it. I'll work my way through it and read a little every night. Your whole family is lovely."

"Thank you."

"They *are*."

"I guess they are. They're the only family I know."

Asha giggled. "You've done well to land where you have."

"You could have a family out there somewhere."

Asha sighed and looked out across the green fields as the descending afternoon sun shone its warm glow upon them. "I don't feel as though I have. Deep down, I don't feel it."

"You'll soon find out. I'm sure."

She looked over at his kind eyes as he faced her. "I hope so."

"And if not, you'll have to stay on in the community."

Asha laughed.

"It wouldn't be so bad, would it?" he asked smiling a little uncertainly at her.

"I think it would be lovely."

"Really?" His face brightened.

Asha nodded. "It's so peaceful and there's no falsity among anyone. Everyone is just as you find them, and so kind and good."

"We're God's people. It's God's love that you're seeing."

"I'd like to know more about God. I've never given Him much thought. I always thought if God was real there wouldn't be so many people suffering."

"There are things that are hard to figure out, that is for sure and for certain. But we know He is real, and that He loves each of us."

CHAPTER ELEVEN

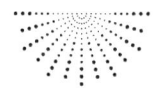

That night, Asha couldn't sleep. As she tossed and turned, negative thoughts crept into her mind. John had told her about *rumspringa*. What if some of the young people coming to the meeting had been on *rumspringa* and knew who she was? How long would it be before she was found out?

Nate would've had to go public by now, and make a statement about why she wasn't going ahead with the tour. Thousands of dollars worth of tickets would need to be refunded. She knew Nate would be furious with her. Wherever he was, she could almost feel his rage reaching out toward her.

She sat up, leaned over, switched on her lantern and reached for her Bible. She opened it and started reading. The words she read said she shouldn't be afraid and to thank God for all He has done. When she turned to another page, her eyes fell to a scripture that told her God would fight her battles. That sounded good to her. After she opened a few more pages and read the verses where the pages had fallen open, her eyelids grew heavy.

She closed the Bible, turned off the lantern, and lowered her head into the pillow.

A change had to be made in her life. Maybe all of the things that had happened to her had been deliberately set in place by God to bring her to know Him? Could she really find peace in her life? Closing her eyes once more, she prayed, promising that she would give her life over to Him if He would give her peace. Not knowing about God or how to pray, she asked God's forgiveness if she was praying in the wrong way.

THE NEXT MORNING, Asha awakened to find the Bible resting on top of her. Had she fallen asleep before setting it on the table after reading it the night before? She recalled all that she had read, and she felt a sense of deep inner peace and understanding. She immediately thought of John. She was excited to see him today, and wondered if he felt the same about her.

Asha couldn't hear any noises and wondered if she was the first to wake. She got ready quickly, putting on the borrowed clothes from Patsy; a plain green dress which, at first, she had felt unattractive in. Now she was used to it because the other women all wore the same sort of dresses.

Once she had dressed she headed to the kitchen. To her surprise everyone was there except for William.

When the three women had greeted her, Gretchen said, "We have cereal on Sundays and we don't do much other cooking."

"Sunday is our day of rest," Stephanie explained.

Jared walked through the back door, and handed a mug to Stephanie with a little head nod.

"Morning, Jane," Jared said.

"Good morning."

Megan explained, "Jared fixes Stephanie her favorite coffee-shop-style hot drink every morning."

"Jah, and he better do it after we're married too," Stephanie said.

"Of course I will," Jared said. "As long as you do everything else in the kitchen."

Stephanie smiled. "That's a good exchange."

"Do you live close, Jared?"

"I live in the quarters by the barn. When Stephanie and I marry, we'll be moving to a small house. Are you coming to the meeting, Jane?"

"Yes."

"Will this be your first Amish meeting?" he asked.

"First of many, I hope," William said as he walked into the kitchen.

Everyone said good morning to him and he sat down at the table with them.

"Coffee, *Dat?*" Megan asked.

"*Jah*, please." William shook cereal into a bowl and then took up the jug in front of him and poured milk on top.

Stephanie said, "This is our last meeting before we get married, Megan."

"*Jah*, it is."

"You're all leaving me," Gretchen said.

"We'll visit most days," Megan said while placing a cup of coffee in front of William.

"I hope so," Gretchen said. "I'll certainly miss you girls."

Soon they were traveling in two buggies to the Williamsons' house. Jared and Stephanie were in one buggy, while Megan and Asha rode with Gretchen and William.

When the buggy stopped, Megan went to find Brandon and Asha wandered over to the house. It seemed they were early, as there were only five other buggies parked.

She looked inside the barn to find the boys still arranging furniture.

"Morning, Jane!" Todd exclaimed as he was lining up chairs.

"Morning, Todd."

"Excited for the meeting?"

"I am, actually. I've never been to a church before, ever. These are all new experiences for me."

"Hi, Jane."

Asha turned around to see John. "Hello."

He pointed to one side. "The men sit on that side and the women on this one."

"Oh, I didn't know."

He laughed. "I figured you wouldn't."

As the people started coming in, she noticed how similar they all looked and not because they were all wearing the same clothes, but because they all had that same certain energy within them.

"Ah, you must be Jane."

Asha turned around as she heard a friendly voice.

"Yes. Nice to meet you." The man had brown hair and blue eyes, and he had a similar build to John's.

"I'm Gabe, John's cousin. I've heard a lot about you. John and I work together when he's not pretending to have a sore leg."

John and Asha laughed.

"I'll remember that. Just you wait," John said.

A young boy ran up to Gabe and held his hand, glancing shyly at Asha.

"Oh, is this your son?"

"No. This here is my little brother, Luke. And somewhere around here is his slightly older sister, Miriam. If you see a little girl running everywhere and creating havoc, that'll be young Miriam."

"I'll keep that in mind."

The families kept coming in and greeting Asha, and she found herself yearning for what they had—a family. They all looked so happy and at peace. Makeup, clothes, and other material objects didn't matter to them. There was no one better than the other and they all greeted each other with such joy and laughter. It wasn't too long before they all took their seats.

CHAPTER TWELVE

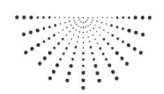

Asha looked around to find somewhere to sit, and Stephanie stood and beckoned her to sit with herself and Megan in the back row. She hurried over, relieved to be able to relax, sit back, and watch the proceedings.

She looked up to see Scott peering back at her from the front row. He gave her a big smile before he turned around.

"Looks like you've captured a heart," Megan whispered to her.

The room went quiet and then she saw John standing at the front. He looked in her direction, gave a small smile and started singing. It was such a beautiful song. She felt goosebumps come all over her body and she closed her eyes to enjoy the song more fully. She opened them to find John once again staring straight into her eyes.

The moment she couldn't stop thinking about was happening again. She looked back into his eyes from across the room. He looked so handsome, and she loved that he also loved to sing. She felt her heart starting to open wider the more she listened. The song finished and John didn't move, he didn't blink, he kept staring straight at Asha. He only moved when the bishop stood.

Feeling her face grow hot, she looked down to her hands.

"Looks like you've captured more than one heart," Megan whispered.

Asha gave her a small smile. John's actions confirmed that he liked her too.

When the bishop spoke, Asha tried to take it all in. She found it hard to understand, but she knew in time it might make sense.

When the bishop finished talking, another man stood and made announcements, and then a third man closed the meeting in prayer. Then everyone stood and moved to the other side of the barn. The boys moved some of the benches away and replaced them with tables, leaving the remaining benches to sit on.

Asha joined Patsy in the kitchen to offer her help. All the women ate on the run while they took plates of food out to the barn and then returned shortly after with empty plates. For the next couple of hours, Asha was in the kitchen helping the women, and she found she enjoyed it.

"You've done enough work for one day, Asha. I've made you a hot cup of tea. Take a seat on the porch or somewhere."

"Thank you, Patsy." She took her cup of tea outside and was surprised to see John on the porch with a spare chair next to him. "I brought you a cup of tea," she said, offering it to him.

John broke his gaze and shook his head as if he'd been off in a distant memory and was coming back to reality. *"Denke,* Jane. That was kind."

She handed him the tea. "Mind if I sit?"

"I'd be happy if you did." When she sat, he asked, "How are you enjoying the farm life?"

"To be honest with you, I love it. I feel at home here, a certain peace that I don't think I've ever felt before in my life, like I was saying yesterday."

"Can you remember anything yet?"

"No. I'm not sure I want to. For some reason, I feel that wherever I came from, I didn't really want to be there. If that makes sense."

He took a sip of tea. "I think so."

"Can I ask you a question, John? And if I am being too forward, please feel free to let me know."

"Sure."

"I noticed the way the woman looked at you in the doctor's office the other day. I am sure you could have been married with a family by now if you wanted. May I ask why you still live at home with your parents? Don't you want your own family?"

Asha saw John swallow hard.

"I-I'm sorry, it's none of my business. I'm too nosey for my own good," Asha said.

John breathed deeply. "It's okay, Jane. I just haven't found the right woman I want to raise my children with, and spend every day with. My family is important to me. I'd rather be here helping them, setting a good example for my brothers. When I find the right someone, sure, I will be happy to marry, but that hasn't happened yet."

Jane gave John a smile and they both stared off into the distance together. Asha couldn't help but feel there was more to the story but she respected John's privacy and didn't let her curiosity get the better of her.

"My leg is better now, so I will be back in the

fields with Gabe tomorrow. I've enjoyed these past few days getting to know you, Jane."

"I've enjoyed it too, John."

"I will see you about the car, though. And take you to see my friend to find out what he can do about the car. That might be tomorrow or the next day."

"Yes, that's good." When Asha looked up, she saw the Grabers heading to the buggy. "It looks like we're going." Asha stood. "I'll say goodbye to your mother."

When Asha came back out to the porch from saying goodbye to Patsy, John was no longer there. She hurried to the buggy so she wouldn't leave them waiting.

"Jane."

She turned to see John walking toward her. "I just wanted to let you know I'm glad you came here."

"Me too. Where did you get to? I came out to say goodbye and you'd gone."

"One of my annoying brothers called me over." He shook his head. "I shouldn't speak about them like that, but they are annoying when they interrupt my time with you."

Jane couldn't keep the smile from her face. She glanced over at the Grabers' buggy to see William give her a wave to hurry up. "I should go," she said as she turned back to John.

"I'll see you soon. Maybe Tuesday, I'd say."

"I'll look forward to it."

As she hurried to the buggy she heard John call after her, "Me too."

It was a refreshing change to meet an open honest man like John. There were no games, no guarding himself against hurt like so many of the men she'd dated, no having to guard herself. There was frankness and honesty in everything he said.

CHAPTER THIRTEEN

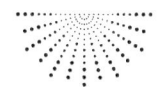

It was Tuesday when Asha saw John again.

Asha climbed into John's buggy and sat next to him.

"He's still waiting for quotes on your car. I'm sorry it's taking so long."

Asha was pleased about any delay that would cause her to stay longer. "That's okay."

"I can take you to see it."

"That's okay. I don't need to see the car, do I?"

"No, I guess not. In that case, would you care to spend the day with me? I've got a whole free day."

"I'd like that very much."

"Good. I've got something to show you."

"A surprise?"

"Yes."

"I like surprises."

Thirty minutes later, he stopped the buggy in a clearing and Asha didn't see anything particularly special-looking around them.

"Where are we?"

"Near a creek." He jumped down from the buggy, and pulled some things out of the back.

When Asha got out, he met her and handed her binoculars while he held a pen and a book in his other hand. "You can use these."

"What are we looking at?"

"Birds. I often come out here by myself and watch them."

Asha frowned. "Really?"

"Don't look like that. I thought it would be boring at first, but then I got interested. My aunt and uncle got me started and it was through their excitement that I got curious."

"Okay. I'm willing to give it a try. What's the book for?"

"I note down anything I see, and if I see something rare, I let the bird society know."

"Ah, and then all the birdwatchers flock here to try to catch a glimpse of it?"

"Something along those lines, but mainly so we

can track what birds are where. It can help with maintaining their species, protecting their breeding spots and things like that. So it's not just for the purposes of seeing an unusual bird."

"Okay." Asha slipped on the muddy trail and John quickly put both hands out to steady her, dropping his book.

When both feet were firmly planted on the ground, she looked into his eyes. There was a brief moment between them before he quickly withdrew his hands.

"Thank you," Asha said.

He leaned down and picked up his book, which now had mud on it.

"Oh no! Your book."

Brushing off the dirt, he said, "It's fine. I was more interested in saving my binoculars."

She looked down at the binoculars she was still holding. "Yes, I knew that. I didn't think you were worried about me."

They exchanged grins.

"Let's go." He strode off. "I know a good place to watch from."

When she caught up with him, she asked, "Will this involve a lot of walking?"

He chuckled. "A little. Do you have something

against exercise?"

"Not really. I haven't done a lot lately." She had to stop herself from telling him how Nate had made her work out every second day.

"What do you know about birds?" he asked.

"Not much. They eat and fly around, and the ones in the city seem to look for clean cars to mess up."

He laughed. "You might learn something today. I'm looking for a Western Grebe. They aren't supposed to be in this area, not this far east, but one of my cousins saw one here last week."

"I've never heard of a Western Grebe. What do they look like?"

"They're a water bird. They look like a swan but with a long beak. Another name for them is a Swan-necked Grebe."

As he talked more about these birds, Asha was pleased that he was interested in nature. Nate had only been interested in money and how to make more of it. The other boyfriends she'd dated had been impressed that she was a famous singer and none of them had any particular interests other than going to nightclubs and drinking. John was different because he took pleasure from animals and nature, and he liked her for herself.

"Well, I hope we see one of the Swan-necked Grebes," she said.

"It's not likely, but you never know what else we might see."

"What are your favorite birds?"

"I like the ruby-throated hummingbird."

"I hope we see one. I think I saw one at your house the first day I was there. You had a special bird feeder there for birds who like nectar. Your mother was telling me about them."

"Did you like it?"

"Yes. The one I saw was so pretty, a beautiful shade of green. It had a red neck and it was very small, and its wings were flapping at a hundred miles per hour."

Asha hardly remembered any birds in the cities where she'd gone on tour except for pigeons, who were treated as pests as they swooped on tourists and nested in inconvenient places such as rooftops and eaves.

The trail opened onto a river and Asha could see that it continued along the riverbanks for some distance. "At least it's drier underfoot here." Movement from the water caught Asha's eye. "What's that?" She saw what she thought was a duck of some kind.

"That's a Green-winged Teal"

"Is it a duck?"

"Yes, a small one. It's proper scientific name is Annas Crecca. Sadly, the population of the American Black Ducks, a larger species, is in decline."

"Now you're showing off your knowledge."

He laughed. "There are a lot of the teals around here. Look, there's another one."

She looked to see another Green-winged Teal waddling on the other side of the bank before it slipped into the water.

He looked up to the sky. "There are usually more birds around here."

"I might have scared them away."

A little further on a bird flew overhead. "What's that? A hawk?"

"Yes. It's a Northern Farrier. A medium-sized hawk. That might be why there are fewer birds around."

"Are you going to write that down?"

"No. I only write down birds I don't normally see."

"I hope we see something rare."

He laughed.

"What's funny?"

"You might be catching the bug."

"The bird-watching bug?"

He nodded.

"I like to watch them. You're right, I might be catching it."

They walked on for another hour while John kept pointing out the different birds and telling Asha what they were.

"Look there. It's an Eastern Bluebird."

"Oh, I love it! Such a beautiful color."

"And they have a glorious voice. A few years ago I didn't see any, and now I'm seeing them more often. It might be that the weather has been warmer these past years. And some of the farmers are building houses especially for them. They are picky about where they nest, and they eat lots of insects so we like them around our farms."

The trail moved away from the water and continued up a hill.

"Have you had enough, or do you want to keep going? I'm not carrying you up that hill."

"Maybe we should head back because of your sore leg."

He laughed. "My leg is better."

"We can't be too careful. If we go up that hill, you might strain it."

"Okay, we'll head back."

When they turned and started back, Asha said, "Thank you for bringing me out here. It's nice to learn more about you and what you like to do."

"It's me who should be thanking you. I usually come here by myself. It's much more enjoyable to be here with you."

She glanced over at him to see him smiling at her.

"Are you hungry?"

"Starving."

"I brought us some food. Just in case you wanted to spend the day with me."

"You did?"

"Yes. Well, my mother packed it for me."

"She's so nice."

"She's a pretty good mother."

When they got back to the buggy, John brought out a picnic basket and handed Asha a blanket. "You find a good place for us to sit."

"Shall we keep the binoculars out?"

"Yes. You never know what we might see."

Asha found a grassy place and spread out the blanket. When they were both sitting down, John opened the basket.

"Now let's see what *Mamm* has packed for us."

"She knew this was for me too?"

"Jah." He pulled out a bottle. "This is ginger beer."

Then he handed her two glasses. "You can pour while I set out the food."

When the food was arranged, Asha saw there were sandwiches, cold chicken, salads and cold potatoes. "I love cold potatoes."

"Really? To me, potatoes should always be hot and mashed."

They stayed there for the next two hours, eating and drinking, and they were so busy talking that no more birdwatching was done.

When neither of them could eat any more, Asha started packing the basket.

"I suppose I should take you back to the Grabers'."

"I suppose. I've had the best day I've had since… Since… I'm not really sure. Maybe the best day ever."

He chuckled. "I hope you get your memory back soon. Well, I do and I don't. I don't if that means you'll leave, but I hope for your sake you do. Then you can reconnect with your family and friends."

"Something tells me I might not have many of those." Asha closed the lid of the picnic basket and tapped it. "There. All done."

Together they drove back to the Grabers'.

When Asha got down from the buggy, John said,

"I'll see you at the wedding. I guess that's the next time I'll see you."

"Yes. I'll see you then. Bye, John, and thanks again."

"Bye, Jane. I had a lovely day."

Asha walked to the house knowing that the longer she stayed there the deeper she was going to fall in love with John.

CHAPTER FOURTEEN

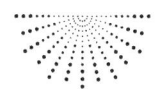

It was the Tuesday night before the wedding, and Asha was having dinner with the Grabers and Stephanie and Megan.

"This is the last time we'll be having dinner like this," Megan said looking sad.

"We can come back here when we're married and have dinner," Stephanie said.

"Yes, you're welcome back here whenever you want."

"We're in for a busy day tomorrow," William said.

As she knew, the next day was the day before the wedding. "Why, what happens tomorrow?"

Gretchen explained, "Our house is too small, so we need a huge covering going from here almost to the barn for the guests in case it rains. And I've only got this little stove, so we need more stoves for the cooking and the heating up of the food. We've got extra hotplates coming."

"And that all happens tomorrow?"

"*Jah*, it'll all need to happen tomorrow. I've got about thirty workers coming to help out," William said.

Asha hoped that John might be coming, but then she recalled he said the next time he'd see her would be at the wedding on Thursday.

Asha asked, "Wouldn't tonight, I mean tomorrow night be the last dinner you have?"

Megan shook her head. "All the workers and their families will have dinner here tomorrow night. It will be fun, but it won't be the same as how it is now."

Asha nodded. It seemed a lot of work to have all those people for dinner the day before the wedding, but she kept her opinion to herself.

"I'm going to have an early night," Gretchen announced. "It might be the last I have for a while."

"We'll do the dishes for you, *Mamm*. You just relax before you go to bed."

"Thank you, Megan."

When the dinner was over, Gretchen and

William left the kitchen, and the girls cleaned up and washed the dishes.

"It must be so exciting for both of you to be getting married. And did it take a long time for Brandon to convert to Amish?" Asha directed her question to Megan.

"A few months. He had to live with an Amish family for a few months first to make sure he was making the right decision, and then he had to take some lessons. And then it was a few more months after that before the bishop allowed us to marry."

Asha nodded. "I suppose that's best. Did he believe in God before that, or before you met him?"

"Yes, I suppose that's what attracted me to him. He did a lot of charity work with the church he belonged to and helped to feed the homeless. Not just feed the homeless and the people who don't have much money, but he became a friend and listened to their problems. That's when I fell in love with him. And he was pleased that he could continue his charity work, because Amish do a lot of that and fundraising too."

Asha nodded. Her impression of the Amish had been totally different before she lived with them.

"Are you thinking of joining us, Jane?" Stephanie asked as she picked up a plate to dry.

"It's crossed my mind. I'm sure I'd be happier here than where I was before. Although I can't remember anything yet, I've got the feeling that I wasn't very happy with the life I was living. And I was probably even trying to escape from it."

"I guess you'll only find that out when you get your memory back."

"I guess so. So, did you finish sewing your dresses?"

Stephanie and Megan smiled at one another.

"Yes, we have," Megan answered.

"We've got all the dresses ready, so we just have to help Gretchen with the food tomorrow."

"And the cleaning," Stephanie added.

"Would I be able to help too?"

"Of course. An extra pair of hands is always welcome."

"Before we do anything else, Gretchen has ordered us to clean the house as soon as we wake up in the morning. That will take a couple hours."

"I'll help with that," Asha said, pleased to be included. She hadn't cleaned in the last few years, but when she was living with her foster families, she'd always had chores to do.

. . .

Wednesday passed slowly. With every new buggy that arrived at the house, Asha hoped that she would see John, and every time she had been disappointed. She tried to push him out of her mind, but every time she heard a bird chirp, she thought of him and the lovely day that they had spent together. Then she'd recall his smile and the way his strong arms had caught her before she fell.

That night Asha stayed up with the girls and heard details about their relationships with the men they were about to marry. She listened to many stories about how they had met them and what they had thought of them. She'd learned how Megan's father had died, and her mother was ill and had no money and had to give her up. She'd heard the story before, and was sad all over again for Megan, that she'd never met her mother or her father. Megan's mother could've been out there somewhere still alive, although Megan said she had a feeling she'd died.

The story Stephanie had was slightly different. Stephanie told of all the trouble she got into and everything she had put her parents through. Now that it was all in the past, her stories were funny, but Asha was certain that Stephanie's parents hadn't found them funny at the time. Now all that was in Stephanie's past and she was about to begin a new chapter of her life with Jared.

Asha was the first of the girls to wake the next morning. They'd all fallen asleep in the same room. She opened her eyes and then felt something across her face. It was an arm. When she pushed it off, Stephanie woke.

"What time is it?" Stephanie asked as she sat bolt upright.

"I don't know. Where is Megan?"

Megan wasn't on the bed and then the girls both saw Megan asleep on the floor. They giggled at the sight, which woke Megan.

"Are we late?" Megan asked sitting up.

"I doubt it. If we were late Gretchen would be in here yelling at us."

"Should I go down and put the kettle on?" Asha asked.

"Yes please, Jane. I won't be far behind you," Stephanie said.

Asha headed into her room and pulled on a bathrobe before she headed downstairs. When she walked into the kitchen, she saw Gretchen leaning over the sink and crying into a handkerchief.

"Gretchen, what's wrong?"

Gretchen turned around and shook her head. "I feel like I'm losing a daughter. That's what Megan has been to me."

Tears stung at the back of Asha's eyes. She would have no one to cry for her when she got married. It touched her to see the bond between Megan and Gretchen.

Asha put her arm around Gretchen's shoulders. "She won't be going far. And then she'll have lots of babies and bring them back here for you to help look after."

That made Gretchen giggle. "I keep telling Elizabeth and Tara to hurry with the babies. Maybe they'll be beaten by Stephanie or Megan."

"That's right."

"We're having cereal this morning because we've got so much work to do. People will be coming soon."

"Cereal's fine with me. I've just come down here to put the tea kettle on the stove."

"It's already boiled."

A very tired Megan and Stephanie walked into the kitchen. Asha was used to surviving on very little sleep, often having to perform concerts while feeling the effects of jet lag.

Two hours later, hundreds of people were there for the wedding.

"Where have all these people come from?" Asha asked Gretchen. There were far more people there than at the Amish meetings.

"Near and far, far and wide."

Asha walked into Megan's bedroom and saw both girls in their blue dresses. It was odd to see people getting married in such clothing.

"You two look beautiful," Asha said.

"Thank you," both girls chorused.

"Is there anything I can do?"

"No, but thank you so much for helping over the last few days. We have really appreciated it," Megan said.

"Yes, thank you," Stephanie said.

"It was lovely getting to know you, Jane. And I'm glad we had that chance."

Stephanie nodded in agreement at what Megan said.

"And you really do look a lot like Asha," Stephanie added.

"Yes, people say that all the time. I better get outside and take a seat."

Asha headed back outside and took a seat on one of the back benches. All the while she was looking for John, but couldn't see him anywhere. She saw Gabe, his cousin, first and then she saw John behind him. John appeared to be looking around and she wondered if John was looking for her. Then their eyes locked and he waved. *Question answered.* She smiled and waved back.

Now she felt like her insides were glowing. Seeing him filled her with peace and happiness.

When all the guests were seated, both girls came out of the house and waited, greeted by their future husbands. Both couples walked to stand in front of the bishop.

John stood and sang a song in German. Asha closed her eyes and listened to his voice. They could sing wonderful songs together. She'd been told that the women didn't sing out in front at the meetings, that only men did that.

When John's song finished, a man who had been standing near the bishop opened in prayer. Then the bishop gave a long talk that went on and on. Asha was so far away she could barely hear what was said. She tried very hard to stop her mind from wandering but her eyes wanted to stay fixed on John.

When the couples were pronounced married, people jumped up to congratulate them. Some of the men started changing the furniture arrangement, bringing long tables to replace some of the benches.

Asha went to help the women in the kitchen, but she was shooed away by Patsy who told her she needed to rest after the work of the past couple days. She headed back to the crowd to find someone to talk with. She didn't want to appear too obvious by going straight to John—the only person she wanted to talk to.

She was helping herself to a glass of soda when she felt someone standing beside her and looked up to see John.

"Hello, John. I really enjoyed your singing."

"Thank you."

"You've got a lovely voice."

"You're going to have to stop complimenting me over my voice or I will get a big head." He chuckled.

"I'll keep that in mind."

"I guess this is the first Amish wedding you've been to?"

"I'd say so. It's doubtful that I'm Amish, or that I've been to a wedding like this."

"If you were Amish we would've heard that there was an Amish woman missing. And you weren't wearing Amish clothing."

"Well, there you go then."

He laughed. "It would make things a lot easier for me if you were Amish."

"Why's that?"

He scratched the back of his neck. "Then I'd only be competing with other Amish men. Not Amish and *Englisch* men."

She laughed. "Do you think men would be competing for me?"

"For sure."

Asha shook her head. "I'm positive there was no man in my life. I wasn't in a relationship before I came here."

"How can you be so sure?"

She put her hand over her stomach. "It's something that I just feel."

He smiled. "I hope so."

Asha spent most of the day in John's company.

CHAPTER FIFTEEN

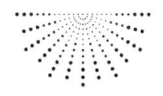

That night, Gretchen was alone in the kitchen and Asha approached her.

"Gretchen, I really enjoyed the wedding. How would someone become Amish? Does your community take people who want to convert? I have heard that you do, that Brandon converted."

Gretchen dropped the plates in her hand back into the sink and turned to face Asha.

"My dear, that is wonderful news! We would love to have you here, but are you sure? When you remember where you came from, don't you think you might want to go back there?"

"No Gretchen, there is a knowing inside me, something telling me that this is where I am supposed to be. This is the life I am supposed to lead.

Even if I have done wrong in the past, I want to make amends for that and I believe everything I have read in the Bible. It's like I always felt something missing, but now I have found it."

Gretchen walked over to Asha, grabbing her shoulders. "I am so happy to hear you say that, Jane. You will have to attend classes to be inducted into the Amish life, if you are serious. You have to study for a few weeks and then be baptized. You need to learn everything about us, and then make a decision after your studies."

"This is great. I want to learn more!" Asha replied.

"Would that have anything to do with a certain young man? A man named John?"

"How did you—"

"I saw the way you both looked at one another today. Sit down and I'll tell you some things about John you don't know." When they sat down, Gretchen continued, "When he was eighteen, he courted Lindsay May. She went on *rumspringa* and never returned. She just forgot about him, didn't even bother to send a letter. Broke his heart, it did."

It all made sense and Asha now realized why he had been so worried that she too, might return to her old life once she regained her memory.

THE NEW GIRL'S AMISH ROMANCE

∽

OVER THE NEXT two weeks Asha and John saw each other every second day. John was delighted when she shared news that she was thinking of joining the community. When she was informed the car was ready, she knew that something had to be done. Should she confess her lies? Or should she stay in her happy bubble for as long as she possibly could, knowing that it would burst? When it burst, she knew it would not end well. How could it, when she'd lied to people who'd only shown her love and kindness?

That morning, she waited for John to take her to her car. Nate's car...

"That's him now," Asha said looking out the window.

"Take a coat. There's mine by the door. It'll be cold out."

Asha stood. "Thanks, Gretchen."

"You can bring the car back here and leave it in the barn if it's ready."

"Thank you. It'll feel strange to drive a car after being in the buggies."

Asha grabbed the coat and headed out to meet John.

"Good morning, Jane."

"Hello," she said as she climbed in next to him.

"Do you mind if we take a detour before I take you to your car?"

"That's fine. You're the driver."

"I will be dropping off some vegetables for my uncle's stall at the farmers market.

"You seem cheery today."

"It's been a good day so far and it can only get better. It's about a forty-minute ride to the markets. I hope that you will enjoy it. You'll be meeting my Uncle Steve.

Asha smiled at John, and then looked at the view. They were passing a frost-covered field that was sparkling in the morning sun.

"John, look how pretty it is."

He looked over. "It is. Mornings are my favorite time of day. Especially the sunrise."

Asha nodded and tried to recall how long it had been since she'd been awake to see the sun rise. "I'll have to try that. I haven't been up that early in a while."

He chuckled at that.

"I'm going to talk to the bishop soon about joining the community."

He took his eyes off the road to stare at her.

"That's great. But, you haven't got your memory back yet. Have you?"

"No. I just know this is what I want."

"Good. I'm happy to hear it."

When they arrived at the farmers market, she noticed small stalls selling fresh produce and various other items. There were many Amish people, and they all smiled and said hello as they walked by.

Asha realized how judgmental and unkind she had been about the Amish. She'd seen them as outcasts and extremists. Now, living amongst them, it all made perfect sense. As they continued walking, she heard a woman's voice from behind, yelling out to John.

They turned around to see Sally from the doctor's office

"John! Hi, how are you?" Sally said, over-enthusiastically.

"I'm good thank you, Sally, How are you?"

"I'm great!" Sally continued, completely ignoring Asha, "I've been speaking with your Amish bishop about joining your community."

Asha narrowed her eyes at her and had unkind thoughts before she could stop herself. Sally was only thinking of joining the Amish because of John.

Then a thought occurred to Asha. Was she doing the same?

"That is good news," John said.

"He said I'm to stay with a family first. Any ideas?"

"Well, Jane here didn't stay with my family, she's staying with the Grabers. I'm sure the bishop will find you a family to stay with."

Sally looked at Asha. "You do look awfully familiar. I can't put my finger on it, but I know I've seen you somewhere before."

Asha felt her heart sink and the anxiety instantly came over her. Surely, she wouldn't be able to tell who she was in a plain Amish dress and no makeup. Asha would never have been seen out in public before without designer clothing and her professional makeup.

Laughing, Asha said, "I get that a lot from people. I think I have one of those faces. You'll be pleased to know that we might be taking those classes together, Sally," Asha advised, trying to change the subject.

Sally's face went blank. "You mean you're turning Amish? Why is that, may I ask?" she enquired looking toward John.

"Jane will be speaking with the bishop soon, Sally.

It'll be good for you both to have each other. We have to get a move on now, " John said as he touched Asha's arm to guide her in the other direction.

At his touch, Asha's heart beat faster.

"Bye, John," Sally yelled out from behind.

"Bye," John said, half-turning back.

"John, how are you?" A large man smiled as they approached his fruit stall.

"I'm good, Uncle Steve. This is Jane, she's new to our community and will soon be taking the instructions," John informed him as he smiled in Asha's direction.

"Ahh yes, Jane, I remember seeing you on Sunday. I have heard a lot about you. I apologize for not introducing myself sooner."

"Nice to meet you."

Uncle Steve gave a small smile, and then he and John continued to talk about produce and the setup of the stall. As they unloaded vegetables from the crate John had brought, Asha took a seat behind the stall and her mind started to wonder again. *What should I do?* If she told John the truth, he would surely see her as untrustworthy, a liar, and all of this would be over in a second. But then she remembered what she read in the Bible.

Do to others as you would have them do to yourself. God forgives all of those who repent.

She knew when she repented and was baptized, all her sins would be forgiven. *It will all work out*, she thought to herself.

The exchanges of smiles continued between John and Asha and she found herself sitting on the stool, getting lost in him once again. He was so tall, so sun kissed, his brown hair and green eyes made him so unusually beautiful and his singing was just as beautiful. She imagined what their babies would be like. She hoped they took after him and had bright green eyes and brown hair opposed to her blonde hair and blue eyes.

As they headed to the garage to see about the car, Asha asked, "Why do you think Sally is joining the Amish?" Pangs of jealousy pricked her heart and she couldn't stop them. She only hoped John didn't know how she truly felt about the woman who was trying to win him over.

CHAPTER SIXTEEN

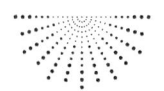

"I have no idea why Sally would or would not do something. I'd rather not think about it, but I am glad if she is doing it for the right reasons," John replied.

"Noted, and what would the right reasons be?" Asha asked, ashamed of herself for the jealousy she felt.

John took a moment to reply. "There could be many right reasons to do it, but the heart has to be in it. A burning desire from within, a knowing that it is the life you want to lead. I respect people who join us. Turning to God and the simple life is not a choice everyone wants to make."

"I should make a time to see your bishop and put things into place."

When the buggy stopped at the car workshop, Asha got out and waited for John to secure his horse. "I can't see any cars," she said when John walked up to her.

"They're all out in the back."

John walked in and asked to speak to Mick, his friend.

A few minutes later a young man in grease-covered overalls headed toward them.

"Mick, this is Jane."

"Hi." He nodded. "Won't shake your hand."

Asha smiled when he lifted up his dirty hands.

"How's Jane's car?"

He sighed. "We're gonna need an expensive part. Sorry about this, Jane. It's not your run-of-the-mill car. I thought we'd be finished. The dent-pounding work and spray painting are all done."

"Good. I'm not in a huge hurry for it."

"Can you pay a deposit today? You'll need to check at the office to see how much it's going to be. You could take it to a Mercedes workshop, you know."

Asha knew the dealership might be able to look up who owned the car. "No. It's fine. You come recommended by John. Do you take a card?"

"Yeah. Jenny at the office will fix you up."

Asha left Mick and John talking while she headed to the office. When she walked in, she heard one of her songs playing.

The woman looked up and gasped. "Are you Asha?"

Asha gave a laugh. "I get that a bit. I'm here to pay a deposit. You're fixing my car."

The woman tapped some keys on the computer in front of her. "Name?"

Asha was pleased the name on her credit card was not Asha. She handed her card over.

"Is it the black Mercedes?"

"Yes."

"Can you leave four hundred?"

"That'll be fine."

The woman ran the card though the machine.

When Asha joined John back at the buggy, John said, "Jane, you have a credit card?"

She'd blown it. Swallowing hard and thinking fast, she said, "I do."

"Then you would know your name." His speech was slow and deliberate.

She looked directly into his eyes. "I don't think I want to be whoever I was before. I feel that deep in my soul. God put me here to find the community.

And to find you." Asha reached out and grabbed his hand.

His eyes fell to her hand on his and he smiled. "What is your name?"

"No. I don't want to be her anymore. Please understand. Just trust me that this is something I need to do."

He covered her hand with his other hand. "I'll trust you, but you must tell me this truthfully. Do you remember who you are? Where you're from?"

"No." She shook her head.

He nodded. "Do you want me to keep calling you Jane?"

"Yes."

"You know it would be easy to find your friends and family now that you know your name from the card?"

"I know that, but I feel I've been put here for a reason."

He smiled. "Me too. I knew as soon as I saw you there was something about you."

"You felt that too?"

"Yes. I think you're the woman for me, Jane. Is it too soon to say that?"

"No it's not too soon at all," Asha confessed, "I felt

that way about you the next day after the crash, when I saw you at your house."

He drove her back to the Grabers' house and she was pleased they'd expressed their feelings, and that she'd gotten out of a sticky situation with fast thinking.

As they pulled up to the house, the smell of freshly baked bread and hot roast pork reached their nostrils.

"Mmm, smell that?"

"Jah. Can you stay for dinner? If it's okay with Gretchen and William?"

"I'd love to.

Gretchen had made a delicious meal of pork, roasted vegetables and salad. Sitting down for a meal with the man she liked and William and Gretchen, Asha felt she had a real family. She knew this wouldn't last and things could very soon get ugly. Asha had lost count how many times she'd lied to John and he was a man with such integrity, she feared he'd never forgive her.

CHAPTER SEVENTEEN

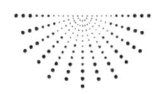

It was a week later, and John was taking Asha back to get the car.

"What will you do with it if you join us, Jane?"

She had to get the car back to Nate somehow. Maybe Jess could catch a bus to see her and then drive his car back. "I'll have to sell it, I guess."

With John alongside her, Asha stepped into the office to pay for the work.

The office lady took her glasses off and said, "The owner of the car has already paid." She nodded to the other side of the office, and sitting there was Nate.

Nate leaped to his feet.

Asha gasped and ran out of the office, followed closely by Nate.

Asha swung around. "Go away."

He stayed back and John ran to Asha. "Jane, who is he?"

She held her head. "No one."

"No one?"

Nate strolled over. "I'm her manager. What the heck are you doing in those clothes?" He laughed at her.

"I'm not going back."

"Jane, what's this all about?" John asked.

"Jane?" Nate looked at John and then turned to Asha. "Yes, *Jane,* what is this all about? And what did you do to my car?"

"Your car?" John looked from Nate to Asha and she looked away.

"It didn't take you long to forget about me, Asha," Nate said.

Asha shook her head. "It's not like that."

"Jane, will you tell me what's going on?" John urged.

Asha looked into his face. He still trusted her after she lied to him. She didn't have the heart to tell him the truth.

"I'll tell you what's going on, farmer boy. This woman's mine, got it? Now go back home and grow your corn or whatever it is that you do."

John frowned and ignored Nate's rudeness and simply pointed out, "Jane's lost her memory."

Nate threw his head back and laughed. "She's a liar. She remembers me all right." Nate nodded to a black car with dark windows. "Get in the car, Asha. Your little vacation has come to an end. Fun's over."

"I'm not going."

"Is this your husband, Jane?" John asked, now looking doubtful of her.

"Her name's Asha, and she's a singer."

"No, he's my manager. *Was* my manager. I'm sorry I lied to you. I just wanted to stay a little longer around you and your family—also the Grabers. I've never felt so wanted or appreciated."

"What a load of rubbish! You don't feel appreciated? What about your millions of fans who buy your music? They've spent millions on you. Talk about spoilt. Thousands of singers want to be where you are. You don't know when you've got it good. Now get in the car!"

Asha looked at John's face.

"Is it all true?" John asked.

Asha hung her head. "Yes."

"You never lost your memory? You were lying to me this whole time?"

Asha nodded. "But I want to stay. I don't want to go back."

John took a step back.

"Get in the car, Asha."

"I can't believe you lied to me. You made it all up."

Nate grabbed her arm and pulled her to the car and she went with him. She couldn't stay, now that she'd hurt John so badly. His eyes told her how much she'd hurt him.

As they zoomed away in Nate's hired car, she asked, "How did you find me?"

"Your credit card was used there. Oh, and thanks for wrecking my car. I'll send someone for it when it's finished." He glanced over at her. "Your sister's worried out of her brain and so was everyone else."

"And especially Julie Rose?"

He growled, "She was never a serious thing."

Asha shook her head. Her peace was shattered and it was back to reality. At least she'd had a small piece of happiness in her life.

"Do you know how many people depend on you? And how many people haven't been paid since you skipped town? There's your sister for one, and your security team, and the list goes on. We all depend on you to put food on the table. Do you know how much money we've had to pay back because you ditched the tour?"

"No, but I'm sure I'm going to hear about every dollar of it."

"And what are you wearing?"

Asha trembled. "Just don't talk. You're hurting my head."

"You're so selfish. After all I've done for you. I made you, and this is the thanks I get."

"God made me and gave me my voice. Not you."

"Ptf!" he spat out. "I had a press conference and told them you were in rehab."

Asha's jaw dropped. "What?"

"Someone caught your outburst on their camera, loaded it onto YouTube and it went viral."

"What outburst?"

"The night when you left, when you attacked me in the nightclub."

"I was trying to get away from you if I remember correctly."

"TomAtoes, TomAHtoes—whatever. Anyway, it's cost us a fortune, you running away like that. You'll have to make it up to your fans or they'll never trust you." He patted Asha on her leg. "You can do that when you get out of rehab."

"I'm not in rehab!"

He shrugged. "You can have a few days off and then we can catch the last few days of the tour, so we'll need to be on a plane to Amsterdam."

"I've quit. I'm not going anywhere."

"We'll talk after you have a rest and after you talk to your sister."

Nate had always been able to make her do whatever he said, but not this time.

Nate delivered her back to the hotel, and before he let the valet park the car, he said, "Get out of those clothes as soon as possible. No one can see you in those." He twisted around and handed her a black coat from the back seat. "Cover yourself with that. Don't talk to anyone and head to our room."

"My room!"

"Our room."

"No. There is no more 'our' going on. I need my own room. We're through!"

"Okay, calm down. I'll get another room; you stay in that one. Here." he handed her the key. "We should go separately and looking like that, hopefully, no one will know it's you. Go now!"

Once she stepped out of the car, she swung the coat over her shoulders, kept her head down and walked to the elevator. Thankfully there was someone just stepping out of the elevator, so she slipped right in. When the doors opened, she hurried to the room next to hers, which was Jess's.

CHAPTER EIGHTEEN

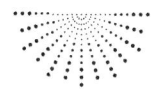

After she knocked on the door, her sister opened it.

Jess grabbed Asha and hugged her. "Where have you been?" She stepped back and looked her up and down. "You look dreadful."

"Thanks."

"Where were you?"

"Trying to escape."

"Did you stay at the Amish place you were calling me from?"

"Yes, and they were lovely. I want to go back and live there."

Jess grabbed both of her shoulders. "You're not being yourself. You're having a breakdown."

Asha wiggled out of her hold. "I'm not. For the first time in my life I know what I want."

"You've always known what you wanted. To be a famous singer, and you are!"

Asha walked over to the bed and sat down. "I've found God, or He's found me, and this life I've got is a fake life."

"You've what?" Jess sat next to her. "What did you say?"

"Found God."

Jess sighed. "They've brainwashed you."

"No, Jess. My brain's been washed."

"Same deal, if you ask me. Where's Nate?"

"Getting his own room."

Jess sighed. "At least that's a step in a positive direction."

"I met a man."

"Ah, now it makes sense."

"It's not like that."

"Isn't it? You've always been manipulated by men. Look how Nate treated you and you put up with it. Now you're onto someone…"

"You have to trust me."

Jess shook her head. "Do you know what you've put us all through?"

"I called you."

"Only once. I've been worried sick and I've hardly slept."

"I'm sorry, but I felt I would die if I stayed here any longer."

"It's not all about you all the time, Asha. Do you know what I've been through, all my life, to try to keep you safe and look after you? Then you run off without a care."

"I'm sorry. Just listen to me, and please try to understand."

Jess sighed again. "Tell me everything from the start."

Asha told Jess everything, starting from seeing Julie Rose with Nate, and running away in Nate's car, about the accident, about pretending to lose her memory so she could stay among the Amish, and about moving to the Grabers.

When Asha had told Jess everything, Jess said, "So, what were you doing? Were you lying to people, pretending to be someone else? What's going on with you? You never lie."

"It's not like that, Jess. The life I have here is not me. I'm not that girl. Everyone back there treats me different and they all called me Jane. I want to be

Jane. I want to be Jane and marry John. Well, that's what I wanted. He won't want me now that I betrayed his trust. I didn't expect to fall in love, it just kind of happened." Asha felt a tear fall down her cheek and Jess pulled her in to hug her

"It's okay. We will work everything out." Jess tried to comfort Asha

"Yes, but Jess, you don't understand. Sally is only turning Amish so she can be with John. I know it and she'll probably end up marrying him."

"You've got to forget it all."

"I can't. I can't."

"Well, why don't we go back there? And you can go back as yourself and talk to John and tell him the truth."

"He already found out the truth from Nate. You should've seen the hurt look on his face."

"If John loves you like you love him, then I'm sure he'll forgive you."

"I don't know how John feels anymore. We never talked about it after he heard Nate's story. He never said anything more after that. Before, he'd said maybe I was the woman for him. Anyway, I've ruined everything." Asha took a deep breath. "I can't go back. I lied right to John's face. He asked me if I remembered anything and I said no."

"Aren't Christians supposed to forgive?"

"Yes, but they might not forget. How will he ever trust me again?"

"Forget about John."

"I can't."

"You didn't let me finish. In your head, take John out of the picture. Would you still want to join the Amish if John wasn't there?"

"Oh. It wouldn't be the same without him."

"He could marry someone else even if you go back," Jess pointed out.

"Oh, thanks. Are you trying to make me feel worse?"

Jess shook her head. "I want you to see things for how they are. You can't change your life for a man. This change must be for you. What do you want?"

Asha bit her lip. Jess was right to ask her that. She had always thought she knew what she wanted—fame and fortune. But it hadn't given her freedom. Fame and money had restricted her and made her life miserable. "I just want a normal life. I don't want to be famous. And what does money matter?"

"Everyone needs money, Ash."

"I'll need to give everything a lot of thought."

Jess nodded. "Good. You can't rush into anything. Get a good night's sleep."

"I walked out on everyone. I didn't even take Patsy's daughter's clothes back to her."

"Just go to bed. Things always look better in the morning."

CHAPTER NINETEEN

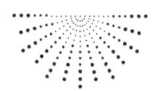

Asha raced into Jess's room the next morning. "I'm going back there. I feel that's where I belong."

"Oh, Asha. Give it more thought than that. You haven't even been home a day."

"My mind is made up and you know that I never change it."

"I know."

"Come with me and meet everyone. Oh, I hope they'll all forgive me."

"Just tell them the truth and say that you're sorry. People only get upset if there's more deception after your apology."

Asha nodded. "You're such a wise older sister."

"I know."

"Will you come with me?"

"Can you really leave everything behind? Give up everything you've worked for?"

"Yes."

"I'll come with you. I want to see what all the fuss is about. We can take my car."

On the drive to Lancaster County, Asha told her sister about the community and the people in it.

"We'll stop at Patsy's house first. That's John's mother."

When they drove up to the house, Jess looked at the farm. "It's beautiful. I can see the attraction to this place."

"Patsy will be the only one home. The others will still be out working. I guess I will speak with her first."

"Okay, Ash, do you want me to wait here?"

"No, I don't think I can do it alone. I need you there."

Together they walked to the front door.

Patsy opened it and when she saw the girls, she smiled brightly. "Jane, what are you doing home? And you've brought a friend."

"Yes, Patsy" Asha said in a small voice, "This is my

sister, Jess. And there's actually… there's something I need to tell you."

Asha noticed Patsy's smile fade from her face as she gestured for them both to come inside and take a seat.

Asha took a deep breath before continuing. "I am so sorry. I don't know how to tell you this after you have been so kind to me and so loving. But I never lost my memory. I remembered who I was this whole time. I just didn't want to go back to my life. I am so sorry." Asha broke down in tears and Patsy rushed to her side

"Please don't cry, child, it is okay. I had a suspicion you never lost your memory."

Asha looked up at Patsy through her tears. "What do you mean?"

"It was just a hunch I had. You didn't seem worried about losing your memory and you wouldn't go to the hospital, or to the police to see if anyone had reported you missing. Do you still want to join our community?"

"I do, but I feel I've ruined my chances in that regard."

"As long as you are sorry for your sins, we forgive and forget. I will just say that it is easier for some to forgive. Others find it not so easy. The boys will be home in a few hours. You will have to tell them and they might not be very impressed with what you say."

The thought of John's reaction weighed heavy on her heart. "John knows."

"*Jah*, he told me."

"I didn't get a chance to explain everything."

"You'll soon have your chance." Patsy said.

While they waited for the others to arrive home from work, Patsy made the girls tea and biscuits. Jess and Asha spoke to Patsy about their lives and the reason why Asha wanted to stay with them so badly.

Before they knew it, the men were walking through the door. Asha's heart sank when she heard the door open. Patsy advised the boys to be seated in the living room, and there Asha found herself surrounded by the whole family. As there were not enough chairs to accommodate all, John was standing across the room, directly in front of Asha.

"So, what's this big news you have to break to us, Jane?" one of the boys asked.

Asha looked at John; he was staring her straight in the eyes with a serious look on his face.

"I don't know how to say this to you all so I just want to start by saying that I've lied to all of you."

She took a moment to stare straight at John before she continued.

"This here is my sister, Jess."

"Go on. Tell them," Patsy gently urged.

"I never lost my memory. I remembered the whole time. My name is Asha, and I am a famous singer in the outside world. I pretended to lose my memory because I don't like my life back home. I don't like being famous. All the pressure, all the stress, all the negativity and all that comes with it. I felt lost, that's why I was speeding so fast that night. I was…" Asha stopped to wipe a tear.

Patsy patted her shoulder, and Asha found the strength to continue. "I was speeding so fast to get away from it all. Then I found you all, and then I found God. I always felt like something was missing in my life. My sister and I grew up in foster homes, but mostly in an orphanage. I have never felt love like you have shown me. All I have ever wanted is a family like yours. When I found it, the only way I knew to hang onto it was to make up lies. I am so sorry."

There was a silence in the room, Asha looked down at her feet and couldn't bring herself to look anyone in the eyes.

Before long, Mr Williamson broke the silence. "Well, are you sorry for what you've done?"

"Of course I am. I say sorry to God every day."

"Well that's good enough for me. You've made your confession and we give our forgiveness. There's not one among us who has not sinned."

"Yeah, Asha, I like your name better than Jane! You can still stay with us, no worries!" Scott added enthusiastically.

Scott always had a way of making her laugh and feel at ease. She smiled in Scott's direction and then looked up at John's face. He was staring at a spot in front of her feet. He looked as though he did not know what to say.

"John?" Asha said in a croaky voice. "May I speak with you in private?"

He nodded and they walked outside together.

John spoke first. "I'm pleased you came back. It shows great courage and so does admitting what you did."

"I'm so pleased you're not angry."

"I believe you did what you did for the right reasons, not the wrong reasons. I know you're a good person. I'm pleased to know that you want to stay. You do want to stay, don't you?" John's body stiffened.

"Of course I want to stay. I came back to ask forgiveness and also to talk to the bishop about joining."

He took hold of her hand. "I was leaving tomorrow to find you. I hadn't told anyone. I'd bought my bus ticket."

"You were coming to find me?"

He nodded.

She knew he loved her as much as she loved him. "Oh, I'm so pleased I came when I did. I might have missed you."

"*Gott* is in control, not us."

"I'm beginning to see that," Asha said.

"He caused everything to happen so we would meet."

"Do you think so?"

He squeezed her hand. "I've never been surer. I've prayed for a long time for a bird-watching partner. It's not much fun by myself."

Asha laughed. "I'll happily be that for you."

"That's what I was hoping you'd say." He shook his head. "I'm so glad you're here."

"I'm so glad you forgive me."

CHAPTER TWENTY

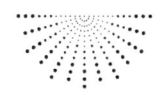

Over the next few months, Asha stayed with the Grabers while she took the instructions. In that time she grew even closer to John.

When a suitable time had passed, the bishop gave his permission to John that he and Asha could marry.

As the wedding drew closer, Jess decided to stay close by, at a place in town to help Asha with the wedding plans. Asha was certain this wasn't the only reason. She suspected Gabe, John's cousin, might have been another reason Jess wanted to be close by.

Every time she mentioned Gabe, Jess seemed a little too interested to hear the sentences that would follow.

Two days before Asha's wedding, Jess and she

decided to go for a walk and have a picnic at the river. Once Asha was married, she knew she couldn't be too close to an outsider, even a birth-family member. The community was her family now.

The sun was shining bright, the birds were singing and the water was babbling and so clear.

"Beautiful, isn't it?" Asha said

"Surreal," Jess added

Asha looked at Jess as she gazed into the distance, and admired how truly beautiful her sister was. Her sandy blonde hair was tied back into a ponytail and she hadn't worn makeup since she'd been staying here.

"You know, I understand why you decided to stay here, Asha." Jess broke her gaze and caught Asha's eyes "It's wonderful here. We never had a family like this, and now you've got one. I'm so happy for you."

"Thank you, Jess."

"But won't you miss the outside world? When they find out you've turned Amish, everyone will be trying to come here to find you, the press will go mad. You'll be all over the tabloids."

"Well, then, let's make sure they never find out." Asha smiled. She knew Jess had a good point, but she simply didn't care. She had learned already that worrying did her no good. She wasn't going to live in fear of other people any longer.

"I'm happy now, Jess, and that's all that matters. Well, I guess being right with God is the only thing that matters. Now I feel I have it all."

"Then I'm happy for you too, Asha. I just worry sometimes… especially about Nate. I know he won't stop trying to make you come back."

"He'll give up eventually." She was surprised at herself, how much she had changed. How much her faith in God had changed not only her beliefs, but the person she was. She had often thought of Nate, and all she felt for him now was compassion. He was stuck, he was sick. She had found a way out, but he was still stuck there. "And what about you Jess?" Asha elbowed Jess, teasing her.

"What about me?" Jess said, pushing her back playfully.

"I see the way you look at Gabe," Asha replied with a wink

They both burst into laughter and Jess made her confession. "Okay, he is pretty cute. I like a strong man in overalls."

They both laughed again

"You know, you'd have to join the community to date him or marry him. We could both stay here together." Asha smiled to herself, hoping that maybe someday her sister might consider it.

"Don't hold your breath, Ash," Jess replied.

When they returned to the place Jess was staying, they saw Nate's black car parked outside.

"Asha, it's Nate."

"What do I do?" she asked Jess, feeling a little panicky.

"Breathe. I will go see what he wants. You wait here."

Asha watched as Jess ran toward the house. What was he doing here? He was going to try to get her back, that's for sure. Would he tell the outside world where she was? There would be a field day here, and the paparazzi would ruin everything. The Amish wouldn't want photographers everywhere.

She had to think smart. How could she keep him on her good side? She heard Jess yell out to Nate in the distance and she watched as Nate turned from the stairs and started to walk toward Jess. She slid down in the seat and watched as they spoke, and then she ducked down lower, out of sight, as he looked in her direction.

Before long, he was back in his car driving away and Jess was running back toward Asha.

Breathing heavily, she said, "It's okay, he's gone. I told him you weren't here."

"What did he say? What did he want? Was he angry?"

"No. He's fine; I think he's just relieved you're alive. He looked sad, like he was about to start crying. I had to tell him that I would take you to see him later on. He's staying at a bed and breakfast up the road. It's your call when you want to go, but if you don't go, he won't leave."

Asha swallowed hard. She felt her anxiety coming back again. Anger started to well within and she pushed it away. "No. We're going right over there now. He's not welcome here or in any part of my life ever again."

"Asha, calm down. I've never seen you so angry. You were so cool, calm, and collected about it all before."

Asha didn't look at Jess. She felt too much anger and pain inside her as she fought back the tears, as the memories of his abusive control over her life bubbled to the surface. "He won't control me any longer," she said as she thought about John and her life here with him.

Jess drove Asha to the bed and breakfast. "There's his car. This is it, Asha. Do you want me to come in?"

Asha thought for a moment before replying. "No. I need to do this on my own. I'll be okay." She tried to reassure Jess, who looked worried.

"Are you sure?"

"Yeah. I won't be long."

She only had to knock on the door once before it opened and she was smack bang in front of Nate.

"Asha! I was so worried" he said as he pulled her tight into his arms. Asha froze. All the hurt, all the pain, all the anger she'd held for him went. He pulled her out at arm's length and looked her up and down. "You're staying here, like Jess said?"

"Yes, I am. I'm sorry, Nate, but I'm never coming back."

"Asha, did you hit your head in the accident? I'm not mad about the mess you made of my car, by the way."

"There's nothing wrong with me. The life I was living was futile and now I've found a purpose for everything."

"That's all very well and good, but people are depending on you."

"I can't live my life for other people. I need to live it for God and for my new family."

"You've gone mad."

"No, Nate, I haven't. I've gone sane." Never in her

life had she stood up for herself like this, and especially never with him. She was proud of herself but in the back of her mind, there was a struggle between right and wrong going on.

"What about us?"

This made Asha feel sick and she laughed in his face, sarcastically. "You never loved me. You loved the money. You cheated on me, you hit me, abused me. I have no love to give you anymore." Asha saw the hurt in his eyes and thought she should just get it over with. She took a deep breath before continuing. "I've met someone, Nate. I'm getting married in two days. Bye, Nate."

"So that's it? After all I've done, you're just walking away?"

Nate pulled on her arm. "Who have you met? Some poor guy that came to your rescue and now you're using him to get back at me?"

"It's not all about you, Nate."

"Okay, Asha, I'll leave you alone. Let's just see how long you last without me. It won't be long until you come crawling, begging me to take you back."

Asha hurried to Jess's car and as soon as she got in, she burst into tears. Jess pulled her into her arms and they sat there hugging each other until Asha felt she could cry no more.

"Ready to go home, little sis?"

Asha nodded. "Gretchen said for you to have dinner with us. Did I mention that?"

"No, that's nice of her."

"You will, won't you?"

"Yes. We can spend more time together that way."

CHAPTER TWENTY-ONE

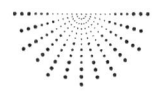

"Girls, we were starting to worry about you. Everything okay?" William asked, giving Asha a curious look when they walked through the door.

"We're fine, and sorry to worry you."

"Asha got caught up with her manager. He still wants her to come back."

"That's why you look so troubled?" William asked.

Asha nodded.

Gretchen called out from the kitchen that dinner was ready. Asha hurried into the kitchen and apologized to Gretchen for not being there to help.

"I'll have no one to help me soon," Gretchen said

with a forgiving smile as they all took their seats at the table. "I guess this was a practice session."

They closed their eyes and said a silent prayer of thanks. Asha's eyes swept across the table, over the salads, bologna, and the mounds of mashed potato. "This is a feast."

"It looks lovely," Jess agreed.

"You'll be married in two days. Stephanie and Megan are married, and I will have an empty house."

"What about me?" William asked with a mock sad face.

Jess and Asha laughed.

"Jah, there's always you," Gretchen replied, barely looking in her husband's direction which made the girls laugh harder.

"We might be getting too old to have more foster children," William said.

"We'll see," Gretchen mumbled. "If *Gott* wills it, we'll have more coming our way. Stephanie came our way and so did Asha."

Asha said, "Maybe Jess might end up staying here and marrying Gabe."

"Asha!" Jess said.

William and Gretchen chuckled.

"It's good to see you smiling, Asha," William said.

"I like having my sister around. And now I've told

my manager face-to-face that I'm not coming back. I feel a whole lot better."

"Good."

"Jess, tomorrow can you take me to John's house?"

"I can drive you anywhere you want."

"Thanks." The wedding was taking place at John's parents' house. John had rented a small house from his uncle for them to live in and it was just a nice walking distance from there to his parents' house.

∽

THE NEXT DAY AT THE WILLIAMSONS' house everyone was eating breakfast when they walked in. John pulled up some chairs for Asha and Jess, while Patsy poured them mugs of coffee.

"The big day is only one sleep away, Asha. You sure you don't want to change your mind? You could marry me instead." Scott teased Asha and she couldn't help but smile.

"It is a tempting offer, thank you, Scott, but I am more than satisfied with my soon-to-be husband," Asha said, expecting John to look up and react, but he didn't.

Everyone else seemed to notice too, and the

room fell quiet with an awkward silence that seemed to make the ants crawling outside sound like elephants stomping.

"Delicious coffee," Jess said breaking the awkward silence.

Asha felt Jess's hand rub her back. She looked at Jess, smiling back at her with a warm smile that said everything will be okay.

Has he changed his mind? Did I do something wrong? After everyone went about preparing the house for the wedding, Asha sought a quiet moment with John.

"Did I do something wrong?"

"Not now, Asha. I don't want to talk about it."

"We're getting married tomorrow. We need to talk about things. If something's bothering you, I need to know."

John looked down into Asha's eyes as he leaned against the barn door. "Maybe it was too good to be true."

"What do you mean by too good to be true? I'm sorry I lied. I just didn't see any other way. I have said I'm sorry for my sins. I've joined the community for you."

"For me? You said you were joining for yourself." He shook his head. "I don't know if I can trust you. What if you run away from me?"

"I won't. We're in love with each other. And I did join for me, but I'd never have found God without you."

"I'm in love with you, Asha. But even your name isn't real, is it?"

"No. I thought of going back to my birth name, but I've been Asha for so long. It's just a name. Tell me if you need me to change back. I'm in this for life. I've made a full and proper commitment, and tomorrow I'll make another sincere commitment to you, in front of everyone."

He slowly nodded.

"What has brought these doubts, John?"

"Something Sally said bothered me."

"Sally?"

"She said you used me and my family, so you could stay here."

"I guess that's what I did in the beginning. John, I am in love with you and I know you love me too. Don't let us go. If I had never lied, if I had never used you and your family, we would never have fallen in love. I wouldn't be here and we wouldn't be getting married tomorrow. Sally has gotten into your head because she wants to marry you, and you know this. Please, John, please?" Asha begged John not to leave her. She dropped to the ground and sobbed. She felt like she was on the ground forever before John's strong hands pulled her to her feet and then into his arms.

"Shhh, shhh, it's okay, Asha. I can't see you like this. I love you. I am sorry, I am so sorry."

Asha was relieved to hear John apologizing. She looked into his eyes and he wiped her tears away. "I guess I let fear get the better of me, and Sally was saying things to me at the wrong time. I shouldn't have listened to her."

"John, we need to communicate; it needs to be you and me, and no one else. No one else should have that kind of power or influence on our relationship—ever. It has to be me and you from now on."

John smiled at Asha. "Okay, Fiancée. That sounds good to me. No more crying for you, and no more fearful thoughts for me. You will believe that I have forgiven you, and I will believe that your words are true."

Asha remembered that his old girlfriend had gone on *rumspringa* and had never returned. "Okay." Asha smiled and buried her head into his shoulder. He was just having a normal 'cold feet' fearful reaction.

CHAPTER TWENTY-TWO

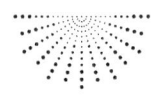

Asha looked at her reflection in the windowpane of her bedroom at the Grabers'. Her hair was tied back and she had a white cap on her head. It was the day of her wedding. Her skin was free of makeup and her dress was plain sky-blue.

She never expected she would get married in a dress showing no skin at all. It was simple, it was plain, and she loved it. She took some time to herself, to review her life. She had gone from having nothing and no money to gaining the world, all the money she could ask for, and then going on to leave it all behind, finding God and a loving husband, finding connection with people instead of connection with her fans.

Caring about others instead of caring about herself. She was pleased with what God had brought to her life. Without Him she would've had nothing. He'd shown her and taught her how to rely on Him. It hadn't been hard to leave everything behind.

There was a loud knock at the door and before she could reply, Jess was bursting through the door

"Oh Ash, you look beautiful! Are you nervous?"

"Hi, Jess." Asha smiled. "No. I'm excited, and you look beautiful too!" Asha looked Jess up and down. She wore a purple dress. It was baggy and covered all of her arms and went right up to the bottom of her neck.

There had been a strong change in Jess too. Before, she would never have been caught dead in a dress like she was wearing, or with no makeup. She knew Jess enjoyed spending time in the community and her best hope was that Jess would join her and call the community her home and her family.

"I love you, Jess." Asha smiled.

"I love you too. Now let's go, or we will be late for your big day."

William was waiting outside in the buggy to take them to John's house.

. . .

Asha walked into the Williamsons' house with William, and her sister followed close behind her. Everyone was seated, ready to watch the wedding take place. It was not the wedding she'd imagined she might have, but she was marrying the best man in the world. A happy-tear spilled from her eye.

Asha looked at John and felt the butterflies going crazy in her stomach. *Breathe Asha,* she thought to herself. Asha looked around; the house was decked out so beautifully with white and yellow flowers. Picked from their very own garden.

She looked back at John; he couldn't keep the smile off his face, and he looked as nervous as she felt. Asha noticed a tear run down his cheek, also.

Everyone stood and a man walked out to the front and sang a song. When it ended, the people sat down. The bishop took over and gave a talk about marriage and how the love in a marriage represents the love God has for His church.

When the bishop finished, he turned his attention to Asha and John. They exchanged vows and were then pronounced married.

The meal after the wedding was set out in the front yard between the barn and the house. It was now midday and the sun was shining brightly. Most marriages, Asha was told were traditionally held at the end of the year after harvest, but that tradition was fading with many of the Amish people no longer living on farms.

Asha and John sat at the wedding table along with Jess and John's cousin, Gabe. Patsy and Joe were at the table closest them and they all chatted cheerfully.

As Asha looked around, she felt her heart open at the love and joy surrounding her. She looked at John's brothers at the next table, now her brothers-in-law, joking around with other Amish teenagers. Smiling, she breathed in the fresh air, taking in the beauty of her surroundings.

When she turned to admire the flowers surrounding Joe and Patsy's house, she noticed Jess and Gabe were deep in conversation.

Mr. Williamson stood and got everyone's attention. "I'd like to thank everyone for coming out today to celebrate my son and daughter-in-law's wedding. We are happy to have Asha in our family. My son, John, we are so over the moon that *Gott* has brought you someone as bright, loving and caring as Asha, and your *mudder* and I pray for His blessing on your marriage and your lives. Thank you for marrying my son, Asha. If you hadn't come along he might've been living at home forever." There was laughter and 'amens' from the crowd and then he sat down.

Asha was struck by the realization that she now had a mother and a father. She couldn't contain her feelings and a tear escaped her eye. John noticed and wiped her tears with his napkin.

"Second thoughts already? It's a little late," John whispered to her.

Asha smiled. "I'm just so happy.

John put his hand over hers and gave it a squeeze. "I'm more happy than I thought I could ever be." He leaned closer and whispered, 'Have you noticed your sister and Gabe?"

"I've been watching them," Asha whispered back.

"Do you think your sister might join us too?"

"I don't know. I hope so."

"This is the happiest moment of my life," John said.

"Are you happier than if you'd seen a Purple Gallinule?"

John threw his head back and laughed. "You've been studying?"

"Yes. If I'm going to be a good bird-watching partner, I have to know what I'm talking about."

"Good. I'd love to see one."

"Me too. It's a miracle we found each other, John. We're perfect for one another. We were from two different worlds and He caused us to find each other."

"I thank *Gott* for you every day, and will continue to thank Him each day of my life."

Asha looked into his eyes and knew that he meant it.

Then visions of the accident flashed through her head. It seemed like it was years ago that she'd run away from her old life and collided with her new one. It was a miracle she had run into John's buggy. She silently thanked God for bringing her home into the fold.

Thank you for reading The New Girl's Amish Romance, the final book in the Amish Foster Girls series.

For a downloadable/printable Series Reading Order of all Samantha Price's books, scan below or head to: SamanthaPriceAuthor.com

RECOMMENDATION

If you're looking for another series to read, you might enjoy the *Amish Love Blooms* series. (6 book series)
Book 1 is Amish Rose.

RECOMMENDATION

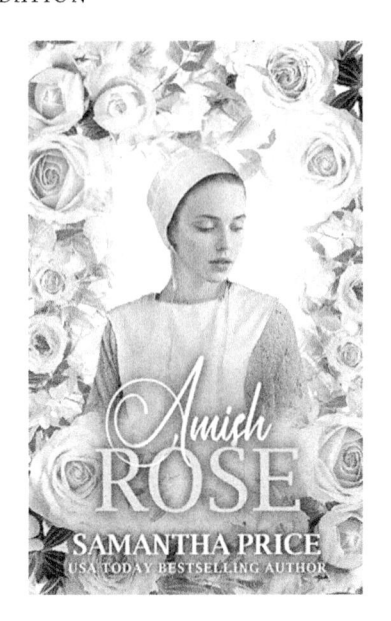

ABOUT SAMANTHA PRICE

Samantha Price is a USA Today bestselling and Kindle All Stars author of Amish romance books and cozy mysteries. She was raised Brethren and has a deep affinity for the Amish way of life, which she has explored extensively with over a decade of research. She is mother to two pampered rescue cats, and a very spoiled staffy with separation issues.

instagram.com/samanthapriceauthor
pinterest.com/AmishRomance
youtube.com/@samanthapriceauthor

Printed in Great Britain
by Amazon